Death Most Unholy

David Q. Hall

Printed in the United States of America
First Printing 2025
All rights reserved.

ISBN: 978-1-948894-46-3

Copyright © 2025 by David Q. Hall

Tree Shadow Press

www.treeshadowpress.com

DEDICATION

Death Most Unholy is the fifth, last, and capstone novel in a series of murder mysteries for which it is the namesake, "Death Most Unholy." It is dedicated to the many loyal readers who have surprised and honored the author with their enthusiasm for what they have dubbed, "the Danny and Tiny" books. I'm immensely grateful for this readership. Thank you for supporting my desire to spin a tale.

ACKNOWLEDGMENTS

Although this author could certainly acknowledge many positive influences and contributors to the writing of this capstone novel, there is one deserving special praise and gratitude. The very first book he was privileged to have published was the first in the "Death Most Unholy" series of murder mysteries, *Death Comes to the Rector*, by Tree Shadow Press, publisher Debra Sanchez. All five murder mysteries, six children's books, and five novellas have subsequently been published by Tree Shadow Press. The author's appreciation and gratitude is boundless. Thank you.

CHAPTER ONE

Mildred Matthison clicked off the phone at her desk in the office of South Presbyterian Church in the South Hills of Pittsburgh, Pennsylvania. She smiled at the fact that it had been one of her favorite office volunteers. She was calling at the end of the last Friday afternoon in July to wish Mildred love and God's blessings for many years to come.

That Irene, thought Mildred, *she's always been so nice. How many times I've called her in a pinch. She'd drop whatever she was doing and hustle over here to fold bulletins when whoever volunteered didn't show up. Or to help me wrestle flower arrangements when a flood of them came in for a funeral on a weekend. It's just like her to want to wish me well on my last day at this desk. What a sweetie.*

After thirty-six years as Church Secretary at South Presbyterian Church, Mildred was retiring at age seventy.

Most of my years on God's green earth, she sighed to herself. *Well, I guess I found my calling.*

She had loved being a church secretary and didn't regret a day of it. *Well, there was that day of Tim Murphy and Mark Stinson's wedding. I would rather have passed on that day. What a tragedy. Mark shot dead on the front walk of the church just after they had been pronounced married.*

She shook her head at that memory and a tear formed in

the corner of her eye. *But that didn't have anything to do with my being Church Secretary.* She rallied and wiped her eye. *I just regret the day.*

After several years had passed, Tim Murphy had been blessed by falling in love again and was married a second time. Fifteen years after the shooting tragedy the congregation had called him to return and become their next pastor. He and his spouse Jeremey lived in a condo not far from the church in the South Hills suburb. Tim was officially "Head of Staff" during Mildred's last year as Church Secretary, but everyone, including Tim, knew full well that Mildred ran the church's day-to-day operations with cheerful efficiency and dedication.

She had never been bossy about it. She just knew all the ins and outs, the history and traditions. She knew every single person who had ever been a member or faithful worshiper. And what every church closet held. Whether paper supplies or "skeletons." Pastors and staff members came and went, but in more than one way, Mildred *was* South Hills Presbyterian Church.

Mildred sighed and turned her thoughts to happier memories as she gathered up her purse and a small cardboard box holding the last of her personal items from her desktop and drawers. She locked the door to the main office of the church and walked the short distance to Tim's study. Then went in and left a thank-you note on his desk for having been such a great pastor and friend. She headed down the hallway toward the back door to the parking lot where her car was parked.

This is a good time to quit, she confirmed to herself once again. *The Personnel Committee can advertise, interview candidates, and hopefully hire my replacement before the fall schedule starts up and things get busier again.*

As she passed the hallway and door to the chancel area of

the sanctuary, she was certain she heard a sound coming from that direction.

What could that be? she wondered.

Everyone else was gone at the end of a Friday afternoon. Henry, the full-time church custodian, didn't work Friday afternoons since he usually had to spend some time at the church on the weekends. So, it couldn't be him. Joanne, the Christian Education Director, had to leave the church mid-afternoons to pick up her kids from school, so it wouldn't be her. Ellen, the regular organist, always practiced on Saturdays, when the sanctuary was usually empty, unless there was a wedding, funeral, or special activity.

Maybe it's one of our members who has keys to the church, Mildred thought. *Maybe Charley Dobbins for Building and Grounds. He had said something about checking that loose bolt in one of the choir loft pews.*

Mildred set down her box, put her purse inside it, and decided she should investigate. She opened the heavy wooden door into the chancel area and walked in.

"Hello-o. Is anyone here?" she called out. "It's Mildred. I'm leaving for the day and need to lock up the church." There was no answer, just an odd intermittent buzzing noise that seemed to come from the back end of the large sanctuary.

What could that be? she wondered.

She crossed the chancel with its red carpeting bathed in colored, refracted light from the stained-glass windows. She walked the length of the center aisle, between curving golden oak pews with red cushions. It was a familiar path that she had taken countless times over all those years, but she couldn't remember ever feeling uneasy about it as she did now.

As Mildred reached the steps up to the back, overhead choir loft – where the organ console was also located – she could tell that the strange, ringing-like noise was coming from somewhere up in the choir loft. She paused and looked around the entire sanctuary another time but couldn't see anyone. There were no signs that anyone had been in there and left anything. She climbed the steps and entered the choir loft filled with pews that matched those down on the main level. As well as folding chairs, music stands, hymnbooks, and other music books.

Now she could tell that the intermittent noise was coming from the region of the railing on top of the wall between the choir loft and the large, open space above the pews for worshipers down below.

It sounds like a timer, she thought, *or probably a cell phone with a timer feature going off. Timing what?* She grimaced slightly with a mixture of amusement and annoyance.

She approached that low wall and brass railing on top of it. Some of Joanne's Sunday School kids had made a banner announcing the coming Church Picnic in August. They had hung it across the wall facing outward toward the chancel and the pews below by attaching it to the railing. As Mildred had walked up the center aisle, she could see that the upper left corner of the banner had a little twist in it, wrinkling the left side of the banner. She considered going back to the office once she left the sanctuary. She could leave a note suggesting that Henry untie and straighten that corner before Sunday morning worship. In the meantime, the pulsing noise seemed to be coming from that very corner of the banner. And as she drew near Mildred thought she spotted something else that was also tied to the railing there.

Why sure enough, it's a cell phone with a strap, tied to the railing and stuffed under the corner of the banner so that it can't be seen from below. Those kids, Mildred shook her head. *Always with the practical jokes. They're probably*

4

hiding in here somewhere, snickering at having lured me in here with their "timer." Yes, time to retire, old girl, but not before one more prank from grade school kids.

Mildred reached the wall and railing hesitantly. Heights had always made her uncomfortable. It made her nervous to reach over and down to untie the string suspending the cell phone. But Henry wasn't there today, and she hated to leave it there just buzzing away. It had gone well past annoying and was just doggone irritating.

Mildred bent over, her head over the railing and her fingers fumbled with the knot to untie the string. She felt a powerful, irresistible push from behind. The small, frail woman was literally catapulted over the top of the railing. It happened so fast and so surprisingly that she didn't even have a chance to look back and see who or what it was that pushed her so forcefully. Her fall was almost completely without hindrance. Except for her right index finger caught ever so briefly in the knot that she had been untying. It was not enough to stop her descent by any means. But it caused her to swing against the little wall for just a split-second before the string snapped and she continued downward.

In that very brief instant, she managed to look up and back to where she had been standing.

You? Her terror-filled mind flashed with instant recognition.

There was another split-second sensation of falling, but almost like flying.

And then the lifeless and soulless body crashed onto a pew below.

* * *

Mildred's warm and giving heart had also been enlarged and weak. It had stopped completely in the nanosecond of her descent, so that she was dead before she struck the wooden back of the pew. In that descent the Angel of Death had swooped through the open space of the sanctuary and intercepted Mildred's instantly departing soul. The angel cradled the soul as she shot through the large, stained-glass rose window at the back end of the sanctuary wall. All time had ceased to apply anymore as Mildred's faithful soul was brought before the throne of God in the timelessness of Eternity and the Kingdom of Heaven. It was not the home that she had supposed she was heading for at the end of that Friday workday in July.

Mildred was Home at last.

CHAPTER TWO

The last Saturday in July the Rev. Dr. Daniel Henriks and his beloved wife, Andrea, were having breakfast at their kitchen table in the East Bay region of Traverse City, Michigan. The previous day had been their last working with Tiny and Angela Jones at *Tiny's Big Security Services* in downtown Traverse City. It had been close to seven years of part-time work with Big Tiny and Angela. Which somehow grew and grew to become often full-time and then some. But Tiny had reached seventy, and decided that it was time for Angela and him to sell the very successful business and spend more time traveling and enjoying each other in leisure.

Danny took a sip of his hot coffee, always decaf from Higher Grounds, the local Traverse City roaster, and smiled lovingly at Andrea.

"Is it going to feel strange, not going into your office as Chief Investigator next Monday?"

Andrea shook her head and laughed, "It's going to feel strange not going into the office any time *today*. I swear, for the last several years it's felt like I was there and engaged in all that investigative work 24/7. Ember here probably wondered why 'Mom' never came home." Andrea reached down and scratched the ears of the elderly English Springer

Spaniel, who wagged her short tail enthusiastically and licked her hand.

"You don't really regret the commitment that Tiny's little 'part-time' job grew into, do you?" Danny asked.

"Of course not. I mean, I would have willingly passed on experiences like having Joe Marichetti Jr. invade our home, bent on killing both of us. Or Susan Sutherland and her serial murders. But working with Angela and Tiny and being so enmeshed in this Grand Traverse area has been the best time of my life. After falling in love with you and marrying you, of course."

"Nice recovery," Danny smiled. "But aside from the extreme danger of those Marichetti and Sutherland experiences, even those got your blood flowing. Admit it."

"Yeah, I admit it. Shoot, I was a career officer in the Michigan State Police, after all. I've never had a discomfort about guns, danger, or lethal criminals. Mostly I feared for *your* safety. It took me so long to find you after having been widowed at such a young age. I would have done *anything* to try to keep you safe."

"Oo-o, you're scoring more and more points here." Danny's smile broadened as he leaned forward to plant a loving kiss on her ready lips. "What say we take your protection and comforting back up to the bedroom?"

The kitchen phone rang.

"You'd swear that damn thing is keyed to our desire for intimacy," Danny grumbled.

"We could just not answer it," Andrea fluttered her gorgeous blue eyes and winked.

And while Danny was tempted to do just that, they *were* expecting a phone call from the Joneses about their celebratory dinner out that evening. So, he picked up the wireless receiver. Andrea sat back and listened to his side of the brief conversation.

"Tim, what a surprise. How are you? What prompts this call?" Danny listened intently. His expression darkened.

"Really? Oh, I'm so sorry to hear that."

"It happened just yesterday?"

"Well, I knew that she was retiring, and I had planned on sending a gift and flowers for her retirement reception at the church next week. Oh, what a shame."

Andrea silently mouthed "Bad news about Mildred?" Danny nodded affirmatively. He continued the phone call.

"Is it too soon to know about a funeral or memorial service?"

"Next Friday?"

"Okay, we'll drive out and be sure to be there."

Andrea nodded in agreement.

"We'll make a point to arrive by Wednesday evening, so that we can see you and participate in the visitation period Thursday evening."

"Okay."

"Thanks ever so much for calling. And again, I'm very sorry for the loss for you and all the church family. Our prayers are with you daily."

"Yes, bye." Danny ended the call.

"How did Mildred die?" Andrea asked with a pained expression.

"Well, it seems to have been a horrible accident. There she was, about to leave the church office after her last day as church secretary for all those years. She probably started when the apostles were still in the Holy Land. She fell from the back choir loft, down onto the pews below. Instantly fatal it seems."

"From the choir loft?" Andrea wrinkled her face. "You never said that she was a choir member."

"She wasn't. At least not in the years that I worked with her at the church. I have no idea what she was doing up there. Tim didn't go into that much detail. But as you remember my telling you, she was single all her life. Said that she felt like a nun, married to Christ and his Church. And her only surviving next-of-kin is her younger brother. He's a recent retiree living in Florida. He and his wife will be arriving on Wednesday also, have the funeral on Friday, and fly back to Florida right away on Saturday."

"What a shock. The two of you were really close. I'm so sorry for *your* loss."

"Thanks, honey. Yeah, Mildred and I worked well together. Especially after the first year as pastor there when I learned time and again that things would always be smoother in the church if I considered *her* way of doing things. And once she was used to the idea of me being in that Pastor's Study, she ran interference for me in a lot of dicey situations. She would almost always give me a heads-up and the answers I needed if the Presbyterian Women, the Board of Trustees, or the Christian Education people, were fussed up and demanding the pastor's head on a platter."

"You mean like Herod's wife and the head of John the Baptist," Andrea snickered.

"Yeah, about like that. But without the sexy, veiled dance on the part of Herodias' daughter."

"Well, it's not too late I can still supply that. We really don't have the office to have to go to anymore, you know." And Andrea gave him her best "come hither" look, for which Danny was always defenseless. She crooked her index finger back and forth as she headed upstairs. Danny had no trouble shelving the tragic news. Their need to make sudden plans to travel could wait until a little later in the day. It turned out to be a Saturday morning with very bad news. But very good "together time."

CHAPTER THREE

The previous Monday a tall, gaunt man passed through the outer gate of the State Correctional Facility. The prison was known to many as "I-Max," due to the maximum-security units and the extremely dangerous criminals who were housed there. The sincere goal of professionals in the corrections system was to try to rehabilitate and aid violent criminals in transforming to become law-abiding citizens. If they were ever able to leave the Ionia facility. But those sentenced to I-Max often became even more hardened, more criminally skilled, and more dangerous during their incarcerations.

It was certainly so with this man who was released on parole after serving seventeen years of a thirty-year sentence. The possibilities of parole could have come earlier for him, but the first few years at Ionia he had been totally resistant and uncooperative with everyone. Guards, counselors, social workers, and virtually all prison staff. Even with the prison chaplain and visiting clergy who came weekly for worship services, Bible study, and pastoral visitations. He had become infamous in the institution for having slugged a visiting pastor who had simply approached him with an offer to "pray for his immortal soul." After that, he became informally nick-named "the Devil's Own," sometimes shortened conveniently to simply "Devil."

Especially in those early, hateful years, Devil seethed constantly with resentment at the injustices, the pain and suffering, the utter wrongness, of what had befallen him. During his lengthy, drawn-out trial process, his attorney-at-law, Steven Reeves, had represented him as well as he could. But Devil had been violently opposed to the entire trial experience. More than once his outbursts and condemnation of everyone and everything, including the judge himself, resulted in at least gagging and restraint, or even removal from the courtroom. Consequently, the counts against Devil kept adding up. The original plotting and conspiracy to commit a crime, false imprisonment or criminal restraint, assault and battery, resisting arrest, assaulting police officers, destruction of private and public property, contempt of court, contempt of the entire judicial process, abuse of jailers and prison guards. Even damaging the correctional system bus when being transported.

And again, the early years at I-Max just added to his record and sentence with more assaulting of guards, fights with fellow inmates, trashing of his cell, sending his cellmate to the infirmary with a broken nose, food fights in the dining hall. The list was threatening to confine him for Eternity itself, were that possible. Law authorities and incarcerated prisoners alike had to agree. "The Devil's Own" was as accurate a nickname as could be. It was a crass joke that his picture was in Webster's Unabridged illustrating the definition of "incorrigible." Bad beyond possibility of reform. Even the starkness of isolation in the darkest pit I-Max possessed was not beyond his abuse. He painted its walls with his own excrement. The warden seriously considered a straitjacket and a padded cell as perhaps the only workable restraint.

There are all kinds of epiphanies and revelations in human existence. They certainly range from extremely religious experiences akin to the classic "St. Paul on the Road to Damascus," described in the New Testament book of Acts. To the more mundane moments of "aha" when someone first realizes that an infernal, tough, plastic package can be easily zipped open if you tear at the little line near the top edge of the package. Devil's epiphany was not so much transforming, life-changing, or problem-solving as it was an event of mere common sense.

One day in his fourth year at I-Max, he had exhausted himself in his rage at everyone, everything, God in heaven, and the very fact of his earthly existence. The epiphany came in his virtually total emptiness. In his nonstop efforts to lash out at everyone and everything, to victimize the world around him with his infernal rage, he realized that he was primarily victimizing himself. There was a psychological logic to that prime result. For he had, indeed, come to hate his very life and being. But a dim light flickered in his consciousness. The rage, revenge, and evil retribution that he sought, like a starving man hungers for food and drink, was not being adequately served by his undisciplined tantrums. Devil realized in that surprise moment that he needed to play the game of rehabilitation. If release from this totally despicable institution was truly possible, it was release and freedom that he wanted. Then he would be able to strike back and destroy his oppressors.

He became a "model prisoner." The warden attributed the sudden change to the eventual effectiveness of modern correctional theory in the judicial and penal systems. The guards kicked it around and decided that they had finally "broken" the wild horse that Devil had become. His fellow inmates discussed him in the common rooms, the yard, the dining hall, everywhere they gathered. They wondered what scheme he was running. Although they were quite glad not to have to punch it out with him so often. The prison chaplain knew that the change was a miracle. An answer to his prayers, of course. The visiting preacher who had been slugged that one day heard about Devil and decided that the faith sacrifice of his jaw had been rewarded with a soul saved. The social worker and psychological counselor chatted and agreed that those difficult sessions had finally borne fruit. The ripple effect of Devil's epiphany rolled throughout the entire facility however erroneous the various conclusions actually were. The nickname stuck, however, too ingrained to be changed. Besides, no one could conceive of calling him "Angel."

When he was scheduled to appear next before the Parole Board, reports were supplied, of course, of his more recent behavior, cooperation, positive spirit, and various actions befitting rehabilitation. The understandably skeptical board members had to ask him to what he attributed this apparent change of heart and mind. And Devil confessed that although others saw him as a changed man, he was still afflicted with anger and resentment. The difference, however, was that he was being helped to manage, control, and even eliminate such feelings and behavior. He did not consider himself "changed" so much as restrained and channeled in healthier ways. And that like any addict, including addictions to violent behavior, he would always be "recovering." And in need of the right kind of help. It was a journey, not a simple destination.

The board commended him on his process, decided that "time would tell." And while they did not just then recommend parole, they were eager to see how he progressed, and what plans and actions for recovery would be forthcoming. Unlike his past experiences, Devil did not erupt and seek the immediate devastation of everyone and everything in the room. He thanked the board members for listening, for their consideration and encouragement. And for giving him the opportunity to meet with them. And although he appreciated the difficulty of recovery, he pledged to work day-by-day for that goal until he was able to meet with them again. He had played the game fairly well, despite their caution and skepticism.

He continued to be the model prisoner, to the extent that he was asked to speak in support groups for newer inmates. He "witnessed" in worship services and Bible studies. He was even asked if he was experiencing a "call" from God into prison ministries. He was now the dictionary illustration for "cooperation," conviviality, and congeniality. All because of an internal epiphany.

The day finally came when he was approved for parole.

As Devil walked away from the prison's outer gate and got into a waiting taxicab, he turned, looked back, and waved at the two guards who had escorted him out.

"Wow," said one, "can you imagine that this day would come for Devil?"

"Not in a thousand years," said the other. "But I really don't think we'll see him back here as a 'repeat.' Naw, he's a free man now and he won't be back."

They were right. But now it would begin.

CHAPTER FOUR

No family member or friend had been there to greet Devil when he walked out of the prison gate. He had cut off contact with any past friends in his complete rejection of everyone in his former life. His well-to-do family had cut him off as unworthy of their love and support because of his crimes.

His autocratic stepfather simply told anyone who dared broach the subject, "I have no son."

His abused mother complied with her husband's commands and turned her back on him.

An older sister regarded him as an embarrassment and a disgrace to the family.

It didn't take long before relatives and friends and social acquaintances of the family learned that the subject of his existence was not to be uttered. His violent behavior had made friendships and alliances in the prison difficult. Even when he had seemingly "reformed," most inmates were leery of whether his "change" would stick well enough to keep their jaws from becoming punching bags.

One of the few exceptions to the wariness of his fellow inmates was a fellow from Northern Michigan who had seemed drawn to him despite his violent hatred of everyone and everything. It had taken about five years, but the backwoodsman from Up North Michigan established some hesitant contact. He wasn't sure just why he wanted to reach out to Devil. But if it had been his nature to be more reflective, he might have realized that Devil reminded him of a kid brother who was also ill-restrained when it came to violent rages and outbursts.

This man became just about his only "friend" at I-Max. He had been released more than a year before and had returned to the North Woods.

I suppose I could look him up, Devil thought as he rode in the taxi. *Ah, but I have unfinished business to attend to in Pittsburgh before anything else.*

So instead of a bus to Northern Michigan, he took the Megabus to the Greyhound station in Detroit. It was a ride of close to three hours, swinging past Lansing, and ended up costing him $88.00, but he bought a ticket for the Greyhound from Detroit to Pittsburgh for Tuesday that only cost him $53.00. It was a direct route, taking about seven and a half hours, and would arrive mid-afternoon. He hated bus travel, but his savings account at the prison was meager, so it was the most economical way to travel. He hated having lost his reliable old Volvo sedan. It had years and a couple of hundred thousand miles on it, but it had still been a quality car, with all-leather interior and the best safety features.

Devil walked behind the Detroit Greyhound station to a dirty alley for a smoke. He had never smoked so much as a single cigarette before being incarcerated at Ionia, but one of the relatively few things he had picked up from fellow inmates was a nicotine habit. He flexed his lean, hard muscles in his arms, shoulders and back. The Megabus had been reasonably comfortable to ride in, but he had felt cramped and was glad to get out and walk.

He thought about his long-planned course of action ahead of him. *I can hardly wait to see the look on the old man's face,* he permitted himself a smirk. *Maybe the shock will kill him on the spot and save me the trouble.*

The tightly wound core of rage that he had so carefully suppressed for so long bubbled down deep inside his psyche, like a volcanic pool that was waiting for enough heat to rise and begin an eruption. He recognized its volatility, however, and capped it quickly.

Stay calm, Devil, my man. He had been called by that nickname for so long at Ionia that he had incorporated it into his own sense of identity. He had even become fond of it. *Stay calm and stay the course. Save the explosion for when it will be the most satisfying.*

He was about to snuff out the cigarette and continue his walk to a seedy motel for the night when a burly figure about his own height emerged out of the dark shadows in the alley.

"Hey man, wha-s-s happin'?" the deep voice addressed Devil. "You got another of those smokes for a brother?"

Calm and composed, Devil casually replied, "Sure, why not?" He reached into the pocket of the light jacket he was wearing.

As soon as his hand was in the jacket pocket, the tough-looking young man with a bandanna wrapped over his head spoke again with a considerably different tone.

"Nah, forget about the smoke. Just give me your wallet. Real slow and easy and you won't get hurt." The dim light of a window in the alley glinted off the blade of the knife that had suddenly appeared in his hand.

Devil didn't even think about the young man's words, the threat of the knife, or anything else, for that matter. The "heat" of the "request" instantly blew off the cap of his psychological caldera. Years of almost daily workouts in the prison yard, the weight room, and push-ups and chin-ups in his cell had made his gaunt frame rock-hard and powerful beyond his appearance. His pocketed hand shot out with the speed of a cobra's strike, striking the young man's nose so hard that it broke at the impact and sprayed blood in a red cloud around his head.

Taken totally by surprise, the fellow dropped his knife and reflexively grabbed his face with both hands as he staggered. His attempted scream of pain and dismay was cut off and stifled, however, by Devil's sinewy left arm across his throat. Applying just the right leverage, Devil grabbed the man's head with his powerful right hand and gave it an extremely violent twist. He snapped the spinal cord in the young fellow's neck. Another valuable lesson learned at I-Max.

Calm and composure returned as Devil lowered the lifeless body to the cracked and dirty asphalt of the alley.

The Angel of Death gathered up the soul of the street hood before his corpse was laid out in an oily puddle.

The flash explosion of rage was gone almost as rapidly as it had erupted. It was with cool dispassion that Devil took one last puff of the cigarette butt he still held in his lips. He gripped the smoldering butt with his right index finger and thumb and snuffed it out in the middle of the forehead of the dead would-be mugger. Without really thinking about it, he put the snuffed-out butt in his jacket pocket to discard later.

"There's your smoke, 'brother.' No need to thank me." Devil enjoyed his little joke, smiled as he walked toward the motel, and easily put the young punk out of his mind.

There had been no one else in the alley. No one had looked out of any window above. No scream had been managed to cause anyone to pay attention. And when the body was eventually discovered and reported to the police by a jogger going past the alley sometime later, investigators attributed the death to "gang violence." Especially since the thug's switchblade was found a few yards away with only his own fingerprints on it. It was safe to conclude that he had been in a fight with one or more rival gang members and had lost badly.

CHAPTER FIVE

The very brief altercation in the alley near the Detroit Greyhound station had a significant effect on Devil. It was almost like a "fix." The calm that had returned to him was less like a lid held on a bubbling pot, as it had been before, and now more like a quiet evening after a thunderstorm. The night in the motel and the bus ride from Detroit to Pittsburgh were relaxing and soothing to him. He was even able to reflect with considerably less agitation than usual about his estranged relationship with his family and relatives.

I must admit, he thought as the scenery sped by on the Interstate 80 turnpike, *in who knows how many generations the family has never had a convicted felon. Oh, felons certainly, including the old man. But never anyone arrested, tried, and found guilty by a jury of his peers. The last seventeen years must have put quite a stain on their reputation and status at the country club and the bridge table. I suppose I should feel sorry for them.*

Contrition and repentance had never taken hold in Devil's own mind and spirit, however. Mostly because of his unshakable belief that *he* was the great and undeserving victim in all that had happened to him. The crimes for which he had been convicted and incarcerated were totally the fault of others. They and an evil God were the ones to be blamed. He might just as well take on the name of the devil, for Satan had to be a more honest spirit than the God who had afflicted him so unjustly. And if there were such spirits as guardian angels in the cosmos and this world, why not guardian demons? One had certainly served him well back in that alley. He smiled again and felt a blanket of peace spread over his sleepy mind.

Upon arriving in Pittsburgh, Devil found a South Hills motel on Clairton Boulevard, State Highway 51, which would serve as a reasonably good location for him. He was able to negotiate with the manager for a deeply discounted rate in exchange for both a long-term stay and his willingness to do cleanup on the grounds and parking lot each day he was there. There was also good local bus service going up and down Clairton. And where the bus couldn't take him, Devil was willing to walk for considerable distances. Walking many laps around the prison yard, the gymnasium, and even the very limited confines of his cell was a habit of many years.

Wednesday, he spent with maps of the metropolitan Greater Pittsburgh area. He knew it well from his youth, having grown up there. He had attended Shadyside Academy in Fox Chapel. He graduated from the University of Pittsburgh in the Oakland area of the city. He worked in the city as an adult. But he had to look at the city in a whole different perspective now. And while he didn't expect a lot of physical changes in the last seventeen-to-eighteen years, he had never been there alone, without a car of his own, and without any school or employment. But he would manage, especially since he had an ironclad plan to get money. And it didn't require robbing a bank or convenience store or some poor dope outside the bus station. Thursday would be his payday.

* * *

The last Thursday in July, Devil put his plan into action. He caught an Allegheny Port Authority bus going into Pittsburgh up Clairton Boulevard, transferred to the Squirrel Hill bus and got off only a few blocks away from his parents' mansion-like house. When he reached the house, he was only mildly surprised that there was a real estate box on a post in a front corner of the yard.

The old man must have finally decided to sell the old barn and make the move to the Florida Keys, he shook his head. *Well, he could live out the rest of his miserable days fanning himself and swimming in Cuban rum. Only $3,000,000.00 for my old home. Sounds like a bargain.*

Devil didn't linger but kept walking while perusing the listing sheet. He didn't want to be spotted by anyone in the house who happened to look out of one of the big front windows. Nor attract the attention of nosy neighbors, although he could probably pass for one of the lawn service workers in the area. He felt certain that his mother would be at the club playing Thursday night bridge. That should leave the old man at home alone, unless he had taken to bringing in one of his bimbos for home delivery. Devil would provide hell to pay after dark that evening. He took off for a brisk hike over to Murray Avenue and Smallman's Deli for a late lunch. He loved the hot pastrami sandwiches that still made the deli famous.

He returned as planned to the old family house after 9:00 p.m. He felt like one of his cat burglar acquaintances back at Ionia. He lurked in the thick shrubbery that landscaped the big, dark red brick house with its four white columns circling the front porch.

No sign of Mom. Well, that was an easy call. She's gone to her bridge game with nary a miss over the last...what, thirty years? If he didn't bring in a bimbo, the old geezer will be in his den, watching the Pirates game on his television, hitting the bottle.

Devil crept over to the back patio. It was a typically hot, muggy, end-of-July evening, but the old man didn't like air conditioning. So, Devil knew that the patio door would be open, with only a locked screen door pulled shut.

No wonder he likes the heat and humidity of the Keys so much. He's willing to let a central air system that cost them thousands of dollars go unused.

It was that thought that spurred Devil to focus more sharply on his mission. He knew that his stepfather didn't feel secure unless he had a substantial amount of cash squirreled away in the wall safe of his den. There he could access it instantly if the zombie apocalypse suddenly came upon them. Or more likely, if he had an urgent lust for one of his bimbos. Devil easily slit the screen down along the outer frame of the screen door and pushed his way in.

It might not have been so easy if the old fart would have been in the habit of setting his fancy alarm system to protect the perimeter of the house with sensors while he or they were in there alone at night. But he didn't think using that investment was really necessary, either. He was totally confident in his Beretta M9 9mm semi-automatic pistol he kept in his den. And later, at bedtime, in his nightstand. Its design went back to the 1950's and had been the Pentagon's choice for a sidearm since 1985, when Devil's stepfather had been in the U.S. Army. He was fond of saying, "It did the job then, and by God it'll do it now."

Devil crept silently over to the door of the den. He had been right about that, too. The old bastard was watching the game, a bottle of Johnny Walker Black and a partially drained glass sitting on his desktop. He liked to watch his ball games from his padded desk chair, swiveling whenever he felt like it to take another sip from his crystal glass. His back was to the door. Devil inched step-by-step quietly on the thick carpeting to the very edge of the desk.

"I'm surprised your choice tonight wasn't a hooker," he announced his presence. His stepfather swiveled around 180 degrees with a look of actual shock on his face. Had the old man been standing, he might have fallen over in disbelief.

Totally surprised, and with his guard down, he blurted, "Frankie, is that actually you?"

The former Father Frank Lewis, defrocked Episcopal priest, did look a good deal different since Harry Wineman had last seen him some eighteen years ago. In addition to the appearance of gauntness and rock-hard muscles, Frank now wore his black hair long, often pulled back in a little ponytail. His eyes were perpetually squinted, as though he strained to see in the darkness of existence that surrounded his life. With a touch of irony that Frank didn't really think about, his old, professional habit of almost always wearing black priest's garb with a small white collar at his throat was continued now by his wearing black shirt and pants, with a light, black jacket. He might have looked almost exactly as he had in his priestly days except that he was minus the white tab in his collar. In some ways, the holy and the demonic are not that far apart.

"Yes, it's Frank," he confirmed for the old drunk. He didn't bother sharing his prison nickname of "Devil." The real devil was sitting in the leather desk chair in front of him.

"Well, did they finally get sick of you and release you from the joint? Or did you somehow manage to escape?" Harry dismissed Frank's attempt to reply as he had over so many years, "No matter, I don't want to know. It's enough that you've broken in here. I'm calling the police."

Harry reached for his cell phone alongside the bottle of scotch.

Frank's caldron of anger did not boil over at that point. He simply reached down like a bolt of lightning and grabbed Harry's wrist, stopping him well before he even managed to touch the phone.

"No, I'm afraid you won't. Oh, you could call them after I leave, I suppose, but you and I have your debt to settle before then."

"My debt? What the hell are you talking about? I'm going to thrash you like the old days, you miserable brat." Harry floundered, trying to get up out of the swiveling chair.

A split-second of deep, suppressed feeling shot up like a plume of volcanic steam from the inner core of Frank's psyche and almost surprised him. It was a toxic, deadly feeling of failure, rejection, fear, and paralysis of his very being. From his early childhood he had been conditioned to accept his total unworthiness and inadequacy, reinforced often with his stepfather's belt. But in that split-second, Frank pushed it back down again. Just as he pushed Harry roughly back down in his chair.

"No, Hairy-nose, that won't happen either." With the ghosts of long ago rising up, Frank reflexively employed the derisive slur he had coined as a grade-school kid for his stepfather. He referred to the fact that it was a lifelong habit of Harry Wineman to let his nasal hairs go untrimmed much of the time, like little brushes sticking out slightly from his nostrils. Frank had been beaten for that nickname, too, so for years he only used it outside of Harry's presence and knowledge.

"Your debt, you old bastard, is all the childhood and innocence you stole from me so many years ago, to say nothing of the abuse you afflicted upon my mother. I should choke the very life out of you this instant, but I need the combination of your precious, secret wall safe to access my payback."

"I'll give you payback," Harry blustered as he reached for his upper desk drawer where he kept the Beretta. Frank knew where he kept it, of course, and as was the case with the cell phone, Harry had no chance whatsoever of getting hold of the gun.

The volcanic magma surged within Frank a bit. He could easily have waited until Harry had the gun in his hand, and then turned it around so that his stepfather shot himself in the face. But he still needed that combination, so he merely hesitated a second until Harry had his hand in the drawer, seeking a grip on the handle of the pistol. Then Devil slammed the drawer hard, breaking two of Harry's knuckles with the impact.

As he jerked his hand out again, Harry screamed, "My God, you broke my hand, you little shithead. Damn," he moaned as he slumped in his chair.

The cap of calm and steadiness readjusted, Frank repeated himself with quiet firmness, "The combination, Hairy-nose."

Along with his mangled hand, the repetition of the childhood slur infuriated Harry. "I'll give you nothing. Nothing, you hear me. You're nothing to me. I never wanted you in the first place, shithead. You were just baggage and trash that trailed behind your mother. I wanted her, and for God knows why, she wouldn't discard you at the curb where you belonged."

Harry punctuated his tirade by placing his good, left hand on the desktop to try to help himself out of the chair, but the eruption blew the top off Frank's calm composure. From the depths of a fiery hell the devil burst out in flames and fury. Devil grabbed the dagger-like letter opener off the desk pad and plunged its sharp point into the back of Harry's flattened left hand. It pierced his hand all the way through with such force that Harry was pinned to the top of the solid oak desk.

A spray of blood became a pool on the desk pad.

His right hand broken, and his left hand pinned and spilling blood, Harry lost all his bluster and defiance, sank down helplessly in his chair, and hung his head down, moaning and sobbing. Devil instantly reasserted his composure, walked around the trapped old man, and reached in the desk drawer to remove the pistol. He checked the slide and chamber, then the clip in the handle, while Harry sobbed and moaned pathetically.

"Oh, not good gun safety, Old Bastard. Fully loaded clip and a hot round in the chamber. Well, at least you had the safety on. Oh, now it's off." He held the muzzle of the handgun firmly against Harry's temple as he slumped face down on the edge of the desk.

"I bet you have a light trigger pull, too, don't you? How 'bout whispering that combination before my finger twitches and adds brain matter to this pool of blood on your desk?"

Thoroughly beaten, Harry painfully whispered the numbers. A little flash of recognition registered in Frank's mind as he realized that Harry had undoubtedly changed the combination to the numbers of the date that Frank was incarcerated.

A demented little celebration, I suppose, Frank permitted himself a hint of a grin. *Well, no more, sick bastard.*

A small mental tennis match was played in Frank's head as he walked resolutely over to the wall safe behind the painting on the far wall.

I should put that round in his head anyway and rid the world, and my long-suffering mother, of this piece of shit. Oh, but she turned her back all those years and acquiesced to his brutality. He spun the dial. *But she was paralyzed and terrorized. But she could have said or done something to break out of that marital prison. And what about her son?*

Once again, he was right. There was almost $180,000 in stacks of mostly Franklins. *Ah, let's see. Ten thousand a year for the last seventeen years, that would be $170,000. Ah, what the hell, I'll just take it all.*

Frank put the taped stacks of bills in the small duffle he had brought with him.

And you know what, old devil? They deserve each other. I'll leave him as he is, and she can step and fetch for him as she's always done. Even feed him, given his recent lack of dexterity.

Frank walked back to the desk where Harry continued in his suffering and moaning.

"I was going to leave you a little bit for a cup of Starbucks over on Murray Avenue, Hairy-nose, but it would be cruel when you can't seem to hold a cup. Oh, they could serve it to you with a straw, I suppose. Well, too late now. I've got it all zipped up and I'm on my way out. See you in hell, you old devil."

"Wait," Harry moaned pathetically. "You can't leave me like this. You have what you wanted. Pull out this dagger and help me wrap up my hand before I bleed to death."

"Hm," Devil pondered that request. "Could you bleed to death there, pinned to your desktop? How is your clotting ability? On any blood thinners for your black heart to keep beating? Aw, there's a chance you won't bleed to death from that wound. Besides, if I unpin you, you may somehow be able to work the phone with your broken right hand. A little clumsy, I'm sure, but you've always been determined in your evil acts. And while the police wouldn't get here in time to apprehend me, since I'll be long gone, why give you the satisfaction of trying?" Devil spat on the pierced hand.

"No, I think I'll just let you reflect on your sins there. Not that you will, of course. I'll let Mom deal with this mess when she gets back from her bridge game. She won't stay after for drinks to keep from having to go home, will she? Aw, probably not. She could be here within...what, an hour or so? You know, when she does get here, if you haven't passed out from loss of blood, you should tell her that it was a home invasion by a gang of vicious burglars. She would never believe that a powerful man like you was overcome by such a worthless little piece of...Ah, but you were, weren't you? Like I said before, go to hell. Whether I see you or not."

Frank slipped out of the house the way he had come in, through the slit screen of the patio door. Then through the thick shrubbery, just in case anyone was looking in the direction of Harry's mansion.

Tomorrow is Friday, he thought as he walked toward the bus stop. *Time to go see that church secretary at South Presbyterian.*

CHAPTER SIX

Danny and Andrea met Tiny and Angela at Trattoria Stella Saturday evening at 6:00. The upscale Italian restaurant had been created in the lower level of the Mercato, in the recently renovated Grand Traverse Commons. It was one of the Henriks' and Joneses' favorites among the many fine restaurants in the Traverse City area. As soon as they were seated, Danny ordered the four a bottle of "Missing Spire" late-harvest Riesling from the Left Foot Charley urban winery located on the opposite side of the Commons grounds.

They didn't bother looking at the menus provided by their server. Andrea and Angela both wanted the Butter Lettuce and Arugula salad, featuring honey-roasted and chilled parsnips, with pistachios and champagne vinaigrette. Danny loved their Berkshire Duroc pork chop, vanilla-brined and char-grilled, Parmesan risotto, with carrots and Ida Red apple slices. And the three of them knew without asking that Tiny would order the pan-seared Georges Bank cod, with fingerling and sweet potatoes, cauliflower, fennel, and lemon. Tiny loved to eat fish, and it had been a long time since Angela remembered Tiny ordering anything other than fish.

As they waited for their orders for their celebratory

dinner, Angela looked around at the attractive and interesting surroundings of the restaurant.

"You know, the few times we've been here before, I've always wondered about this big, old building. It seems like the restaurants and shops down here in this lower level were built in basement catacombs or something, with the doorways and passageways and the rough walls."

Andrea, a native of the Traverse City area, knew the history well and was quick to share.

"As a matter of fact," she explained, "when first built in the 19th century, the Commons buildings had been the Northern Michigan State Asylum for mentally ill patients. It received its first patient on November 30, 1885. Eventually it became known as the Traverse City State Hospital. When the hospital was closed for good, the State of Michigan had planned on demolishing its numerous pressed white brick buildings. But instead, the old facility was renovated building by building and transformed into multiple uses. Including condominium residences, a bookstore, a furrier, specialty shops, restaurants and candy shops, all kinds of cherry products, of course. Hence the name 'Mercato'."

Danny jumped in and interrupted.

"From the Italian, I believe. At least I remember the famous Mercato Centrale in Florence, Italy."

"Okay, yeah," Angela replied. "Now I remember from my African studies class back at Cal State Los Angeles. The largest open-air marketplace in Africa is the Addis Abba Mercato in Addis Abba, Ethiopia. Market or marketplace."

"Much like our dinner menu descriptions," Tiny laughed good-naturedly. "Kinda gussied-up fanciness for this old ghetto boy. Oh, but scrumptious-looking fish." His eyes widened appreciatively as the server arrived and set the big dinner plate down in front of him.

"Well," Andrea said, "the renovation and development has

certainly been well done. What could have been dilapidated and dismal facilities only good for destruction has become one of the premier spots in this whole Grand Traverse area."

"Hear, hear," Danny joined in again. "A toast to the Commons, the Mercato, and especially to your sale of the security business, your retirement, your upcoming world travels. And we hope many more fine dinners and other occasions for the four of us."

"And we need to include Bill and Mary Swanson again," Angela suggested. "She told me at church last Sunday that she's going to join Bill in retirement at the end of this year."

"Really? Yet another of us looking forward to a major life change," Andrea commented. This must be the year for big moves in life and work."

Danny frowned. "And that would have included my old church secretary at South Presbyterian back in Pittsburgh, Mildred. Were it not for her death yesterday."

"Mildred died? I remember her," Tiny's jaw dropped slightly. "Oh, man, I'm really sorry for you. You two were really close. What happened?"

Danny explained. "After, gosh, probably thirty-five, maybe thirty-six years, Mildred had also decided to retire at the age of seventy. Yesterday was to be her last day. The folks at South Presbyterian were going to have a congratulations and thank you reception for her after worship tomorrow morning. Big sheet cakes, cookies, punch, coffee and tea, with cards and gifts. You know, standard church celebration stuff. I had been emailed about it and arranged for a floral arrangement and gift donation from Andrea and me. I was shocked, then, to get a phone call at breakfast this morning from Tim Murphy."

Angela grimaced "I'm afraid I can't think of poor Tim without remembering his wedding day, when his new spouse, Mark, was shot to death in front of the church."

Tiny added to the interruption and reached around Angela with a big, comforting arm, "And you were severely wounded, sugar. I had never been so worried and weak in my life. At least not until that hit man, Gino Marichetti, had you under his gun down there in Southern Illinois."

Andrea and Danny joined in their expressions of pain and discomfort. Angela shook herself slightly and said, "Sorry. Please, tell us about Tim's call."

"Okay, well, Tim thoughtfully called to let me know that Mildred had just closed up the church office at the end of the afternoon yesterday. But before going out the door she went into the sanctuary. Investigating authorities told Tim that it looked like she climbed the stairs into the back choir loft to try to untwist the corner of a banner across the face of the choir loft wall that Sunday School kids had made to promote the annual Church Picnic next month."

"Apparently, she leaned out over the low railing to reach the cord tied to the banner, leaned too far, lost her balance, and plummeted down onto the pews below. Tim said the police have labeled it a tragic accident."

"Oh, Danny, that's horrible. So sad." Angela reached across the table and put a comforting hand on his arm.

Despite so many years of dealing with all manner of deaths, tragic accidents, terminal diseases, grieving spouses and parents and families. Despite having officiated at hundreds of funerals, memorial services, vigils and tributes to departed lives, Daniel Henriks stifled a small sob of his own, and then rallied and went on.

"Andrea and I had not planned on going back to Pittsburgh for Mildred's retirement reception. Frankly, my presence there would have distracted from her celebration, with people wanting to spend time with their old pastor. But her death changes things."

Andrea spoke up, "I told Daniel that of course we should

go to her funeral service to honor her memory. And to offer love and support to her younger brother who will be there from Florida. We'll offer our condolences in person to Tim and others who will grieve and miss her so much."

Angela turned her head toward Tiny and whispered in his ear.

"That's a great idea," Tiny became enthusiastic. "Now we don't want to intrude, but how would you like company for that trip next week to Pittsburgh? Ang and I would love to add our support. I knew Mildred, too. And we've been talking for the last few years about my taking Angela back to see my old stompin' grounds on the Hill and, shoot, throughout the whole city."

"And he really means Stomping, too," Danny brightened and kidded his best friend. "Angie, when I first met this guy, he was probably the most feared...and respected," he hastened to add as Tiny glowered at him playfully. "*Really* respected, street gang leader in the whole Hill District. Why, who knows how many heads he stomped on back in those days," he continued to jab at Tiny.

"Those *bad* old days," Tiny insisted on clarifying. "I became a changed man long ago, a law-abiding citizen and businessman now, totally reformed. The darling poster boy of the Pittsburgh mayor's gang reform/clean up the streets/remove the riffraff, social program." He tilted his head, put his massive mitt up to his cheek, smiled as broadly as he possibly could, and looked like he was mugging for some photo shoot. Angela shook her head and laughed at her senior citizen/yet always-the-little-boy husband, waving her hand at him weakly as if it could make him stop. Andrea and Danny joined in the fun and pretended to be snapping cameras as he posed.

Once they settled down, Danny spoke up again.

"I'm sure Andrea would agree, I think that sounds great,"

Andrea nodded in complete agreement. "Another road trip for the Henriks and the Joneses, but this time without murderous Susan Sutherland or Sarah Brand or who knows how many professional hit men. Despite the sadness associated with Mildred's passing, we can have so much fun back in – no stomping now, big fellow – our old hometown."

Mostly, not completely, but mostly, settled down, Tiny asked, "When do you plan to leave, and how long do you plan to be there? And are you now thinking I'll drive you in my Town Car? And with that little, black chauffeur's cap that you got me. But which you know damn well is too small and so it balances on top of my head like, like some organ monkey's kepi?" he blustered with exaggerated indignation.

"Hey, you look good in that cap. I love it," Danny countered.

Andrea and Angela jumped into the verbal fray.

Andrea turned to Angela with mock seriousness and asked, "Isn't that like the old pillbox hat?"

To which Angela quickly replied, shaking her head and her hands in front of her, "No, no, ah, damn, sister, what do they call those little caps? Well, anyway, there should be one of those elastic chin straps to keep it from falling off that high perch atop his bushy head."

Danny had thoroughly lost his composure by now, laughing uncontrollably and practically falling out of his chair, but the girls kept rolling with their imagery. Without really responding to Angela's "chin strap" comment, Andrea continued.

"Oh, oh, I know, it's 'fez'. Like a fez perched up there."

"No, girlfriend," Angela waved her off. "The *fuzz* is all that gray bushiness that sticks out from under the cap."

Danny doubled over and disappeared for a time under the edge of the table, hooting and literally snorting uncontrollably. Tiny had tried valiantly to keep eating his delicious cod filets and somehow act aloof and above all the ribbing at his expense, but with the "fez" and "fuzz" jabs he involuntarily spewed some of his fish out of his cavernous mouth onto his plate and then roared with delight.

Damn, he smiled to himself as he tried to keep the rest of the chunk of fish secure in his mouth, *we sure have fun. This is going to be so much fun, going back to Pittsburgh together.* In his more serious, more reflective moments, Will "Tiny" Jones knew full well that he could easily have had his life cut short with a violent death years ago somewhere in the underbelly of the Hill. Instead, God's angel had watched over him, blessed him, and graced him with so much love that it could serve for all of Eternity. And eventually it would.

CHAPTER SEVEN

Before the four left their fun dinner, that night they coordinated their plans and decided that they would leave the first Wednesday in August to drive to Pittsburgh. They would easily make the trip and arrive in the late afternoon, checking into the Omni William Penn Hotel, a high-end hotel in downtown Pittsburgh. They had thought about staying closer to South Presbyterian Church. But they discussed all their respective ideas of where they wanted to go and what they wanted to do in the Greater Pittsburgh area while they were there. Staying downtown in the fine, old William Penn seemed like a central location.

Tiny phoned ahead before they hit the road from the Henriks' East Bay home and made a dinner reservation at the Terrace Room at the hotel for 7:00 p.m. Wednesday evening.

The Terrace Room advertised that they were *"Pittsburgh's premier, historic dining experience."* And yes, they would serve him fresh Alaskan halibut, while surrounded by their historic molded-plaster ceiling overhead, accented by carved walnut arches and columns. There was a large, back wall mural that was famously entitled, *The Taking of Fort Pitt,* from the frontier battle going back to the French and Indian War days in the 18th century.

* * *

Thursday morning Danny drove a rental car east and south to South Hills Presbyterian Church, leaving Tiny, Angela and Andrea at the William Penn. Tiny wanted to drive his Lincoln Town Car up into the Hill District to show Angela around more of his old neighborhood. They invited Andrea to go with them. Danny had an appointment with Pastor Tim Murphy for 9:00 a.m. in his study at the church.

After a hearty greeting and pouring a couple of cups of coffee for the two of them, Tim had Danny sit at the round table he kept at one end of the study for small meetings. Smiles and "how are you's" and initial chit-chat finally transitioned into Mildred's tragic death and the funeral service planned at the church for tomorrow, Friday at 10:00 a.m.

Tim, who had always had a good, close working relationship with Danny when the latter was his Head of Staff, spoke as a friend as well as an old colleague.

"I was already going to miss Mildred when she retired, but to think that I...we...will never even see her again. Well, you know better than I, Danny, words fail even the most articulate preachers." He shook his head and wiped at the corner of his eye with his fingers.

Danny, too, felt a bit of a lump in his throat, but replied, "I was trying to think, and I believe I knew Mildred for over a quarter of a century. She was here in the church office when I first arrived to become the new pastor, served as our secretary and mother hen the years that I was here, during the next pastorate, and then how long since you were called back to become pastor?"

"Over a year, about a year and a half. I know it's an old cliché, but they threw away the mold when God made

Mildred. What a great woman. Although it *really* was time for her to retire from her church duties."

"Because she had reached seventy, you mean?"

"Well, that, of course, the long hours and weekly grind of church business and activities weren't so easy for her anymore at her age. But she had frankly grown increasingly dissatisfied with the new directions the congregation was taking in association with my being called here to head things up."

Danny was curious and a bit incredulous. "You don't mean that South Presbyterian was becoming a More Light church, advertising an upfront, open inclusion of all people, regardless of sexual orientation, color, ethnicity, ancestry, no distinctions, or divisions? Mildred always struck me as perfectly okay with our belief that God created all people as equal human beings, as equally loved children of one Divine Parent."

"So far as I could tell," Tim replied, "she was. She was certainly affirming and supportive to Mark and me when we became engaged and had our wedding plans for here. And also when Jeremy and I arrived. I think what bothered her most was the inevitable drifting away of many old, established members. It wasn't just the same-sex marriages, or our transitioning to become a More Light congregation soon. It was the demographic changes that were transitioning the surrounding neighborhoods. Going from the old – I really don't like to say it – 'lily-white,' middle-class suburbanites to much more of a racial and ethnic mix that is more reflective of the demography of the nation as we move farther into this 21st century.

"Oh, and it's not that she objected to the changing neighborhoods. It's more that we 'lost' the old, traditional Presbyterian constituency, if you will. Many people and families that moved in near to the church were Roman

Catholic, conservative and evangelical church members, independent and non-denominational believers. And especially among the younger adults, non-attenders of any church worship or fellowship."

"I have to admit," Danny confessed, "that I don't follow the demographics of the Greater Pittsburgh area like I used to. But I do remember that taken as a whole, the ninety distinct neighborhoods of Pittsburgh used to be comprised of close to ninety per cent whites back in 1950, with something like twelve per cent African-Americans, mostly on the old Hill and a few other places. Folks of Asian or Hispanic ancestry and identity hardly registered at all."

"Exactly right, good memory," Tim smiled. "And while whites still make up a majority, it's shrunk to, oh, about two-thirds, with African-Americans more than doubling. And Asians and Hispanics together approaching ten per cent before long. And some of the people who have moved into areas around the church are classified as white, with European ancestry, but are Eastern European, with traditions in the Orthodox communions. As I said, a much greater mix of people than half a century or more ago. And while we vigorously welcome all, the irresistible move of the church's membership has been downward, pretty much year-after-year. We count less than half of the membership that was here when you were the pastor and head-of-staff."

"Another thing I know," Danny added, "is that Pittsburgh is still the 20th largest metropolitan area in the United States, rated 'most livable city in the country' by different sources. But the overall population has declined at least slightly in the last few years. I suppose it's been a combination of the national and local economies and the trending to the so-called 'sun belt' of more southerly states."

"Right again. And getting back to Mildred, after all her years as Church Secretary, and having served here in more prosperous times, as much as she loved South Presbyterian and its good people, I think the time was right for her to pack it in. Oh, forgive me. I really didn't say that right."

Danny put him at ease. "Don't worry, I know what you meant," he laughed. "But you did remind me of her tragic death. Would you mind if I looked at where it took place? I mean, I have some trouble understanding just what happened."

"Sure, come on, I'll walk you in there."

Within a couple of minutes Tim and Danny were standing at the back pew where Mildred's body had struck. A repair crew had already been in there at the start of the week to erase any scratches, marks, or possible blood spots in the area. A new pew cushion had replaced the old one. Danny looked up at the choir loft above and saw the Sunday School kids' banner that still hung on the low wall facing the front chancel area. Especially since there had been a brief investigation into the cause of Mildred's death, the small twist in the left upper corner of the banner had been left as it was.

"I don't mean to exhibit anything like morbid curiosity, but I'd also like to go up there and look. I'm still trying to wrap my head around just what happened and how."

"Feel free," Tim encouraged him. "But if you don't mind, I think I'll dash back to my study. I still have preparations for tomorrow's funeral, as well as getting my sermon done for Sunday morning. You remember how that is. You have more than enough to do as it is, and then funerals and weddings and special events gobble up hours of your time when you're trying to meet your usual demands and deadlines. Oh, but please don't lean out over that low railing."

"I remember and shudder," Danny laughed, "at what it was like before I retired from pastoral ministry. They always said that 90 percent of your members wouldn't have any idea of what you did in ministry 90 percent of the time. Or have it occur to them how much time and effort you had to put into things like weddings and funerals. So, by all means, go. And I'll be careful up there."

Danny climbed the steps and made his way over to the low wall and railing. Despite Tim's cautionary words, he looked over and down with some puzzlement and reflexively scratched the back of his head a little.

This really doesn't seem right at all. He thought and wrinkled his brow. *I don't understand how this could have happened.* He walked back down the steps, out of the sanctuary, and back to Tim's study, where he knocked on the door.

A "come on in" responded, and he stuck his head in through the door opening.

"Just a quick question, Tim, if you don't mind, and then I'll be out of your hair. You had said in your initial phone call to me that it appeared as though Mildred had been up there trying to untie and untangle the corner of that banner."

"Yes, that's what the investigating detectives told me. In fact, when she lost her balance and fell, her index finger apparently was caught for just an instant with the cord wrapped around it, and then the weight of her body jerked the finger free, and she continued her fall." Tim visibly shuddered. "I hate even to think about it, poor Mildred. Why do you ask?"

"Oh, I'm sorry. You remember how I am, just compulsive and obsessive and a neat freak. I couldn't help but notice that the banner was still twisted slightly at that corner."

"Oh, right, I'll have to ask Henry the custodian to fix it before tomorrow's funeral. Thanks for reminding me."

Danny pulled his head back out of the door opening and closed it. Tim listened to his retreating footsteps.

I suppose old Danny's right. That banner should be

straightened before the funeral. Somebody or other would probably look up at it and think about fuss-budget Mildred up there, trying to straighten it and then falling to her death. Still, it seems odd that Danny would make a point of it. Well, he means well, I suppose.

CHAPTER EIGHT

Danny caught up with Tiny, Angela, and Andrea for lunch at Len's Diner in Oakland, close to the famous Cathedral of Learning on the campus of the University of Pittsburgh. As soon as he found a parking place in the lot next to Len's, he joined the three on the sidewalk where Tiny was pointing out nearby sights and giving information about Pitt.

"And Tony Dorsett. You remember him, All-America running back here at Pitt and star NFL player. He used to come up to the Hill for fried chicken with me at Willie Stargell's shop and...Hey, there's Danny."

The four bustled through the door of Len's, where everything was done fast. Seat you, take your order as you were descending into your seat. Cook it fast. Serve it in a virtually unbroken motion as it came off the grill. Present the check. Take the money. Thanks for coming to Len's. And you were out the door while still munching on your last bite. But the burgers and sandwiches were great. The two couples talked fast as their orders were being prepared.

"So how was it up on the Hill?" Danny asked Andrea and Angela.

"Very interesting," Andrea replied. "Your best friend – Big Tiny here – walks the streets there like a celebrity."

"Yah," Angela agreed. "It was that way the first time he

took me there. And everyone still seems to remember him, despite how long he's lived back up in Northern Michigan."

"And how was it meeting with Tim after all that's happened?" Andrea asked Danny.

"Also interesting," he answered, but with a bit of a grimace. "But troublesome might be a better word."

Andrea looked concerned, "Not any friction with Tim, surely. You guys always got along great. He isn't bothered about you showing up for Mildred's funeral, is he?"

"Oh, no. No. That's not it. Here's the deal. I asked about Mildred's death, of course. But I also asked, politely, if Tim minded if I looked in the sanctuary where her fatal fall occurred. He was very agreeable about that and walked me in there."

Tiny perked up. "I know what's coming here. You thought the circumstances of her death were suspicious. Just like you doubted that Bill Brand's was really a suicide. That's it. Isn't it?"

Andrea jumped in again, "But honey, from all we've heard, Mildred's horrible death was an accident. She lost her balance and fell. The police didn't even find a hint of anything else to suggest otherwise."

Danny held up his hands under the onslaught of their reactions. "Okay, okay, both of you are right. Maybe it was just a tragic accident. But I'm afraid Tiny's right, too. The circumstances really don't add up for me. Now before you say it, all three of you, I'm fully aware that I carry around some paranoia in my mental duffle bag. Along with my obsessive-compulsive traits, my 'neat freak' tendencies, and my irresistible urge to be a 'buttinsky' when I should leave things to the professionals. But in my defense, you must admit that we've had quite a history of stumbling across suspicious deaths and murders. And more than once, mind you, people really *have* wanted me dead."

Andrea recognized the truth of what her beloved husband was saying. She also recognized the futility of trying to shut down where he was going regarding Mildred.

"Go on," she said with as much love and understanding as she could muster, "tell us what you saw and think."

Thus encouraged, Danny laid out his concern. "All those years that I knew and worked with Mildred, one of the reasons we meshed so well together was that we had some of the same tendencies and preferences. Like me, she was pretty compulsive about her routine. When she had put things away at the end of her workday, she would gather up her purse, her jacket or coat if she had worn one, whatever she was taking home with her. And then she would lock the Church Office door and head straight to the parking lot for her car. It was almost unheard of that she would forget something and go back and unlock the office again."

"So, with the situation that's been described to us, if she had felt fussed up about the kids' banner on the choir loft, she would have gone in there first, taken care of that, and then gone back to pack up and leave. It was just her way. Once she was headed out the door, she left. Another thing, even if she altered her routine – say with a jogged memory that she should adjust that banner – it would have bothered Mildred to set down her box of things right there in the hallway before going into the sanctuary. She would consider that a potential hazard for someone to trip over."

"But Tim told you that she was there alone at the end of last Friday," Andrea pointed out. "There wasn't anyone there who could have tripped over the box."

"I know. I know," Danny agreed. "But see, that was Mildred. She wouldn't have set her box down like that. It would have bothered her to do it. Unless something caused her to go against her usual nature."

Tiny spoke up again, "Oh, man, I'm afraid that sounds

awfully thin, brother. Maybe she just didn't feel like carrying the box back to the office to set it down. Or out to her car and then come back to the sanctuary."

"Sure, maybe," Danny agreed. "But that's not the half of it." He leaned across the diner's table in their booth and spoke more intensely. "I remember well that Mildred was afraid of heights. Almost terrified sometimes. She wouldn't go up a couple of steps on a step ladder to get something off a high shelf. As much as that twisted corner on the banner would have bugged her, she would have left a note for Henry to take care of it, please. Something or someone made her discard her routine, suppress her fear of heights, and put her in a vulnerable position."

The other three thought about what he was saying for a second, and Angela spoke up again.

"Danny *could* have a point. My old Aunt Maisy had a fear of heights. 'Acrophobia' it's called."

Tiny interrupted, "I thought that was fear of open spaces, crowds, stuff like that."

Danny couldn't help himself. "No, that's 'agoraphobia.' From the ancient Greek, 'agora' being marketplace or public square."

"Our biblical scholar," Andrea smiled and shrugged.

Angela finally continued. "Yah, so it's acrophobia. Mildred had an irrational, pathological fear of heights."

Danny was still stuck in his scholarly mode. "There's also 'areoacrophobia' – fear of heights in open air high places. And simply 'areophobia,' fear of drafts and such..."

Andrea put a hand on his arm, "Back to Mildred, dear."

"Well, there is one other thing that I've wondered about. But let's talk about that later. Our server is casting dark looks in our direction. This is Len's, and we're not being fast about getting out of here and freeing up our table."

CHAPTER NINE

Friday morning the Henriks and the Joneses arrived at South Presbyterian Church shortly after 9:00 a.m. for the period of visitation before the funeral would begin at 10:00. They queued up with the other well-wishers and mourners until they reached Mildred's brother and his family to express their condolences and support. The line continued past the open casket, where the four stood briefly and looked down at the lifeless and soulless body of Mildred nestled in folds of satin.

Danny did so unobtrusively, but he leaned down very slightly and peered at Mildred's right hand as it was folded with her left hand across her chest. Despite the application of makeup by the mortician, he could see bruising on her right index finger where it had been caught in the cord of the banner as she fell and was swung for a split-second against the choir loft outer wall until she broke free and continued her fall.

That's a really narrow bruising, he thought. *That cord tying the banner to the railing is pretty stout, more like a light rope. You'd think that just about her whole finger would be discolored with the yank it suffered.*

The funeral service began promptly at 10:00, just after the funeral director and his assistant closed the casket and retreated off to the side of the sanctuary. Pastor Tim Murphy made appropriate comments of sympathy to Mildred's brother and his family who were seated in the front pew, just in front of the pulpit. The brother was invited up to the pulpit to share some comments about the life and love of his deceased sister.

Then a lifelong friend of Mildred who had gone to high school with her in Mount Lebanon, Pennsylvania, delivered a brief eulogy. She praised Mildred as having been a devoted Christian, a dedicated servant of Christ and his Church, and "probably the holiest person I've ever known."

That designation stuck in Danny's thoughts as Tim proceeded with the *Service of Witness to the Resurrection* from the Presbyterian Church in the USA's 1993 Book of Common Worship. Danny himself had usually preferred the briefer liturgies contained in the 1960's Worshipbook, but he knew that Tim resonated to the more ecumenical and traditional services that had been incorporated into the Book of Common Worship. The formal service lasted the better part of an hour, including a final hymn, and then Tim came down from the pulpit, faced the closed casket on its wheeled stand, and concluded with:

"Holy God, by your creative power you gave us life, and in your redeeming love you have given us new life in Christ. We commend Mildred Matthison to your merciful care in the faith of Christ our Lord who died and rose again to save us, and who now lives and reigns with you and the Holy Spirit, one God, now and forever. Amen."

As Tim led the casket and the procession of mourners down the center aisle, out of the sanctuary and through the opened outer doors of the church, Danny obsessed on those words: "Holy God...Holy Spirit...Mildred, a holy person..."

But her death was most Un-holy he thought. *I really think she was murdered. Pushed out of the choir loft and down to the pews below. Could it be? Or am I just transferring my own experiences onto poor Mildred?*

Tim had adopted the role of a cantor just before those final words. Singing, "Give rest, O Christ, to your servant with all your saints, where there is neither pain nor sorrow nor sighing, but life everlasting."

Maybe I should chalk up my suspicions and uneasiness to my own "baggage" and let Mildred lie in eternal rest and peace.

But that would have been most unlikely for the Rev. Dr. Daniel Henriks. At his core, he knew that he would pick at the circumstances of her death until he was proven either wrong...or terribly right.

After the casket was carried to the back door of the black Cadillac hearse and loaded, a typical funeral procession wound its way to the memorial garden where Mildred's body was interred. Tim also led the brief, graveside committal service, but he graciously asked Danny if he would like to say a few words and lead a final prayer. In keeping with the traditional tone that Tim had set for the occasion, Danny waited until the coffin was lowered into the grave, and as Mildred's relatives grabbed handfuls of dirt and cast them onto the coffin below, he recited from memory: "In sure and certain hope of the resurrection to eternal life, through our Lord Jesus Christ, we commend to almighty God our sister Mildred Matthison, and we commit her body to the ground, earth to earth, ashes to ashes, dust to dust. Let us pray..."

* * *

The short committal service was concluded within fifteen minutes. Those who had come out to the cemetery in the funeral procession were invited by Tim to return to the church for a light luncheon and time of fellowship. It was close to 12:30 by the time that Danny, Andrea, Tiny, and

Angela got back to South Presbyterian. They lingered in the church parking lot for a few minutes, looking for Tim, Jeremy, and Mildred's family members to return from the cemetery.

Tiny expressed his bad memories of that day when death crashed the wedding of Mark and Tim at the church. Sarah Brand's brother, Ken Romano, had fired a shot from the top of the hill opposite the church, aiming at Danny. But he struck Angela in the upper back, nicking her lung. The 168-grain boat-tail bullet had passed through her without hitting bone and ended up killing Tim's new spouse, Mark.

"I didn't think all that much about those memories and feelings when we planned on coming here for Mildred's funeral," Tiny admitted. "But Sugar..." he turned and looked down lovingly at his beautiful Angela. "Being here now and remembering, it was an unspeakable horror seeing you lying over there, bleeding and unconscious."

"Big boy," she smiled and looked up into his broad face, "believe me, it's harder on you than it is on me. I don't really remember the shot and lying there. The impact and accompanying shock must have knocked me right out. The first thing I remember was waking up in the emergency room, wondering what had happened and why I was there."

"Well, if you did remember," Danny suggested, "maybe it would be helped at least a little by the fact that the surrounding scene here has changed as much as it has. It doesn't look like it did the day of that wedding. Remember how the hillside across the street, opposite the church, was all brush and scattered trees? How it went all the way up the slope a couple of hundred yards to the old Seven-Eleven and its parking lot up on top?"

Tiny agreed, "It really has changed a lot. Now that hillside is all developed. Condo units over there to the left, that apartment building to the right. You can't even see the old

Seven-Eleven up there, assuming it's still there. Feels like development is closing in on your old church here, Danny."

"Yeah," Danny said, "And I'm sure they did a lot of digging out and filling in to build those buildings over there. They better hope it all holds when heavy rains, winter snows, and freezing hits over the years."

"That's a problem?" Andrea wondered.

"You better believe it, dear," Danny affirmed. "Remember, Tiny, oh, how many years ago, when days of rain brought in by the remnants of one of those hurricanes washed away fill dirt in this area? The compacting during construction wasn't able to hold it in place solidly enough. And rows of houses started sliding down the slope, breaking free of their foundations and crumbling apart?"

"You bet your ass I do," Tiny nodded grimly. "Some millions of dollars in insurance money, lawsuits, political battles. If it hadn't been so tragic for the folks affected, it could have been almost funny. Like Danny said, ladies, rows of houses were affected. And the houses built on the heavily filled sides of new streets were sliding down into the houses that had been built below them on dug-out stretches. Ironically, the houses sliding down had nothing underneath them but thousands of cubic yards of fill. The houses being crashed into by the avalanche of dirt and houses had only a few inches of dirt, then solid rock, underneath them. Picture an unstable terracing of the hillside," he said as he made a stepping motion with his hand.

"Got it," Andrea visualized. "Much like the way it looks over there."

Just then the funeral director's limousines carrying Tim and his spouse, Jeremy, and Mildred's relatives pulled into the parking lot. Everyone went in and down to the Fellowship Hall for the luncheon. There was the predictable buffet of ham and cheese sandwiches, potato chips, tossed greens and gelled salads, platters of cookies and several pies and cakes.

Not included was the big week-old sheet cake that remained in the church kitchen freezer and was decorated with icing on top, "Congratulations, Mildred, from a Loving Congregation." The President of the Presbyterian Women and her lieutenants decided to leave it in there, but later carefully scrape off the icing lettering. They would serve it on Sunday in cut up pieces for coffee hour fellowship after worship. Only they would know that it had been intended for Mildred's reception the previous Sunday.

The luncheon was finishing, and people were expressing their condolences to the family again before leaving. Danny caught Tim in a moment when no one was engaging him in conversation, and he seemed to be heading out himself.

"I just want to thank you Tim, for the good service for Mildred. And, of course, for including me at the graveside. It wasn't at all necessary, but I was glad to do it."

"And I was very glad to have you here. In fact, I know that many of our old members were happy that Andrea, your friends, and you, came. It was a very thoughtful gesture and witness to Christian love on your part. I wish I could stay and spend more time with you folks, but I have a meeting to get to in the church library at one o'clock." He shook hands with Danny and left.

Danny watched Tim leave the Fellowship Hall and go out into the hallway to head upstairs to the library. But just outside the door of the hall, Tim encountered a man who seemed to be looking for him, and they headed up together.

I think that's Todd Hickman, Danny thought. *I haven't seen him for years, ever since I served on Pittsburgh Presbytery's Property and Finance Committee when I first got here to be the pastor. I wonder if he's still one of the key trustees for the assets of the presbytery. And what would he be doing at South Presbyterian for a Friday afternoon meeting? He lives up in Fox Chapel and will have to fight late Friday traffic to get home for supper. Well, not my concern. But I am still concerned about Mildred's death. Or possibly her murder.*

Danny rejoined Andrea, Angela, and Tiny at their table.

"So, Tim had to leave?" Andrea asked. "I was hoping we'd get a chance to talk to him some more."

"Yes, he said that he had a previously scheduled meeting up in the church library," Danny explained. "Well, we might as well get going ourselves. I think that Tiny wanted to drive up to the North Side and swing by the Steelers' facilities before it got too late on a Friday afternoon."

Tiny smiled, "I've never had a chance to visit the Great Hall there and see the memorabilia they have on display from all the great players and teams for the Pirates and the Steelers. If you three don't mind having that as one of our sightseeing stops."

As the four headed out toward the parking lot, their route through the church took them past the library. Just out of curiosity Danny hesitated enough to glance in the window of the closed door. He could see Tim at the table, intensely looking down at some papers. But he was not at the head of the conference table, where the pastor often sat to moderate church meetings. That chair was occupied by Todd Hickman. Another attendee at the table was an old, familiar face from among the elders of South Presbyterian, Bernie Recker. And Alice Nelson, a very capable businesswoman who owned her own real estate agency and had been a leader in the congregation back when Danny had been pastor. There was also a younger man who Danny didn't recognize.

Probably a more recent member whom I haven't met.

As they reached the outside door to the parking lot, standing just outside was yet another familiar face for

Danny.

"Jenny Kennedy, how are you?" Danny greeted the older lady who had always been either an elder or a deacon or women's group leader over many years.

"Daniel, how wonderful to see you," she beamed. "And this must be your lovely bride from Northern Michigan. Where are you from, dear? Taylor City I think I heard."

Andrea smiled and warmly shook Jenny's offered hand. "It's Traverse City, actually, and Daniel and I live in that Grand Traverse area now."

"Traverse City," Jenny repeated. "I bet there's some history behind that name." She leaned forward and explained, "I used to teach history in high school in nearby Baldwin, so I always like to learn more about my favorite subject. But maybe another time. So horrible what happened to poor Mildred, falling to her death on her last day here at the church."

"Words don't suffice," Danny agreed, and he proceeded to introduce Tiny and Angela to Jenny.

"How marvelous to meet all three of you. I'm not surprised that Daniel here is accompanied by two beautiful women and such a magnificent specimen of a man. It probably takes all three of you to keep track of him," she winked. "Did you play football, Mr. Jones? Not that all large men are football players, of course."

Tiny confirmed that years ago he had played as a defensive lineman for the Pitt Panthers, until he was injured.

"Say, Jenny," Danny changed the subject. "You've been active in the church and the presbytery for what? Decades? I'm sure. Did you happen to see Todd Hickman arrive and head into the church while you've been out here?"

"Why yes," Jenny said. "I was chit-chatting with a couple of my Dorcas Circle friends here in the parking lot before they got in their cars and drove off. And while we were standing here, Todd arrived, parked, and hustled in, like he was late for something. Why do you ask?"

Danny couldn't help looking a bit puzzled and explained, "Well when we walked by the library just now, it looked like Todd was presiding over a serious meeting that involved Tim and some church leaders. I'm afraid I'm just being nosy. It's none of my business what they are doing."

Jenny leaned even closer to him and virtually whispered. "Well, I'm not privy to what's going on, but something's up, dollars to donuts. Todd's been a wheeler-dealer in Pittsburgh Presbytery for about as long as I can remember, and now he's the Chair of Property and Finance. That makes him the head trustee for the business of the presbytery. If he's here on a Friday afternoon, leading a meeting in our church, you can bet it's not because he wanted to buck the traffic to visit the South Hills in the summer heat and humidity."

"Kinda what I was thinking," Danny agreed. "Thanks, Jenny, and may the angels watch over you."

"They always do, Danny boy," the widow waved as she headed to her car.

Back in Tiny's Town Car, with Tiny behind the wheel, headed toward the North Side, Andrea was curious.

"Why that little discussion about a Friday afternoon meeting in the church library?" she asked Danny. "We Presbyterians are always meeting, meeting, meeting the least little thing to death. What's scratched an itch for you about that?"

"I know. I know," Danny agreed. "You remember what I've always said about us Presbyterians and our compulsive meetings."

"We all remember that one, Danny," Tiny shot a fake complaint to the back seat. "'Cause you tell it over and over. How we can forget about biblical images of hell as burning lakes of fire or stark isolation in 'outer darkness.'"

"Yah," Angela jumped in, "you've always said that the true metaphor for hell and eternal damnation is a perpetual committee meeting in which nothing is ever accomplished."

"And I believe it. I truly do," Danny added. "I've been in so many meetings. Elders, deacons, committees, sub-committees, task forces, local church, presbytery, synod, General Assembly, ecumenical, inter-faith, community organizations, all levels of government. The list itself feels infinitely long and spirit-crushing. But assuming that this afternoon's meeting at my old church is intended to accomplish *something*, I wonder what it might be."

"Well, you can put it out of your mind, my love," Andrea assured him. "It's none of our concern. We were just there for Mildred and her family and friends."

Danny told her that she was absolutely right, but the "itch" was still there. And for some unexplainable reason he wondered if it had anything to do with Mildred's demise. He couldn't help himself. He just had to try to find out more about what was going on at South Presbyterian.

* * *

Back at the church, Frank Lewis had watched the funeral service from a dark, recessed corner of the back choir loft where Mildred had plummeted to her death. When the mourners had gone off to the committal at the cemetery, Frank had watched the Henriks and the Joneses get into the Town Car and join the procession. He made his way down to the Fellowship Hall and inquired cheerfully of the ladies in the kitchen as to when the luncheon would begin.

"I certainly don't want to be rude or seem impatient," Frank said cheerfully to them, "but I'm afraid I have to leave soon and get back to work."

"Well, why don't you just help yourself to one of these

ham and Swiss sandwiches, some chips and a cup of coffee," one of the kitchen volunteers encouraged him. "And there are plenty of cookies over there on those platters."

Frank thanked them graciously and put a sandwich and chips and cookies on one of the plates he took from the stack. He went off to a quiet corner of the hall to eat. He contemplated his next move.

I was right. The funeral of that old church secretary brought Danny Henriks back here to Pittsburgh, along with his wife and those friends of his. There were too many people around before and after the funeral to approach him. But who knows how long they'll be here before they drive back to Northern Michigan? I need to get a fix on where they're staying and look for my opportunity.

He lingered outside in a back corner of the parking lot and hunkered down in the used car he had obtained now that he had plenty of cash at his disposal. He had found an independent used car lot with a serviceable, late-model Ford Focus where the dealer practically salivated at a cash deal. He napped lightly until he was awakened by cars returning to the church from the graveside service. Before long he spotted the Town Car and watched as Tiny parked and the four went back into the church for the lunch buffet.

Now, I just have to tail them when they come out and leave again. But I want to catch him alone.

Frank followed them to the Northside and watched as they pulled up to the Steelers' facilities. He waited for them to come out again so that he could follow them to wherever they were staying.

* * *

After a visit to the Steelers' facilities' Great Hall where all four of them enjoyed seeing the exhibits of all those old sports greats, Tiny drove them back downtown to the William Penn. As they walked through the lobby from the parking structure, Danny spoke to Andrea privately for a moment.

"Would you mind terribly if we let Tiny and Angela do a little sightseeing on their own tomorrow morning? And I'd appreciate it if you would tag along with me while I do a little checking up on things there in the South Hills."

"Still needing to scratch that itch, are you?" Andrea teased him. "Sure, I can tolerate a little alone time with you, I guess. Besides, knowing you, my dear, not much this side of heaven or hell is going to prevent you from sticking your nose in where you feel compelled to go."

"You're so understanding," Danny smiled and reached out and gave her a big hug as they walked behind the Joneses. "I promise. Just some time tomorrow morning."

Andrea doubted that, but she would go along. If Daniel wanted to do some investigating, she was growing curious, too. *What does he think might be going on at the church, and what could it have to do with Mildred?*

* * *

After the four had entered the hotel and headed up to their suite, Frank approached the main check-in counter and spoke to a stylishly suited young woman behind the counter.

"Oh, dear," he puffed slightly, "I'm late rejoining the Henriks party. I think I just saw them go up. Can you help me, please?"

"Sir, I can't send you up to their suite, or give you their suite number, or share any private information. I'm so sorry," she said politely but firmly.

"I understand," he assured her, "and I greatly appreciate the fact that you guard your guests' privacy and identity information. In fact, I think the William Penn is one of the best places to stay in the entire Eastern United States. I actually want to book a room so that I can stay with the Henriks party while they're here. Could you be so kind as to help me with that?"

The clerk was beginning to relax and warm up to the tall, well-dressed man who was so courteous and charming. "We have several fine rooms available right now. Please fill out this registration card and include all the highlighted lines with your personal information. Including your vehicle, and, of course, your driver's license and credit card."

Frank fumbled and felt around pockets and appeared flustered to the young woman. "I seem to have left my wallet in the car's center console for security. But I know the make, color, and license number of my car. May I complete the registration as far as I can, check in, and then come back to give you my license and credit card? I understand and accept that the room will not actually be mine until I satisfy your registration requirements. But I really need to catch up to the Henriks' party. Oh, and I'll be staying as long as they are."

A bit too relaxed and off-guard by now, the clerk, said softly, almost to herself, "Until next Thursday, then. Okay, Mr. Brand. But what I'll have to do is hold on to this registration until you return with license and credit card, after which I can give you your key card. But don't worry," she added with a cheerful smile, "I'll be sure to hold your room until all is complete."

"Thank you so much for your help and understanding, ah, Melissa. I'll be back shortly."

And that's what I wanted to know. They're here until Thursday next week. No rush then, plenty of time and opportunity.

Frank had no intention of staying at the William Penn. He

went a few blocks away and checked into a shabbier hotel where the desk clerk didn't care a bit about proven identity or credit cards. It was a cash-on-the-spot kind of establishment that often rented rooms by the hour. In fact, when Frank had slipped the clerk an extra twenty in appreciation for his help, the burly fellow smiled and responded cynically, "Thanks. Far as I'm concerned, for a twenty-dollar tip, you can be the devil himself."

Funny you should say, Frank thought and smiled to himself. *I think I'll go up, put my duffel in the room, and see about this companionship that is available here on an hourly basis. Now that I have a fix on the Henriks party and their schedule, I'll get back to them, actually him, later.*

CHAPTER TEN

After a sumptuous breakfast at the William Penn's first-floor dining room, Tiny and Angela took off to go to the Pittsburgh Zoo in Highland Park for the morning. Assuring them that Andrea and he would catch up to them there for lunch, Danny and Andrea drove across the Fort Duquesne Bridge to the Pittsburgh Presbytery office on Allegheny Boulevard in the Northside of Pittsburgh.

"Won't the presbytery office be closed on a Saturday morning?" Andrea wondered.

"According to their regular schedule, yes," Danny confirmed. "But when I called yesterday afternoon, I managed to reach Dennis Lyons, the General Minister of the presbytery. 'General Minister' is what they call the head administrator here, what we refer to elsewhere as the executive presbyter or general presbyter. Anyway, he remembered me from my days in South Hills and Pittsburgh Presbytery. HeAlice said that he was going to be in his office this morning, trying to catch up on paperwork, as well as to prepare for..."

Andrea interrupted, "I know. Meetings. Meetings. Meetings."

"You got it. Plus, I guess he has to go to the General Assembly headquarters in Louisville, Kentucky sometime next week, and he wants to get as much done as he can before the trip. Anyway, he said that he would certainly have time to see us if we wanted to stop by."

Danny buzzed at the main door once they arrived at the building, and within a few seconds Dennis confirmed that it was the two of them and buzzed them in.

"Danny Henriks, welcome back," Dennis greeted him as they came through the door of the office. "And welcome to Mrs. Henriks, also. Or do I remember correctly and it's Sergeant Henriks?"

"Please call me Andrea," she replied smilingly. "And it's no longer Sergeant Henriks of the Michigan State Police. I retired several years ago."

"Please help yourself to the pot of coffee I made in the office here. I'm the only one in the office this morning, so I'd appreciate help in drinking it up."

The three settled down at a small conference table in the Dennis' office with their cups.

"I wish we could take more time to catch up on everything that's been going on in your lives, and mine," Dennis said rather apologetically. "But maybe you could get to whatever you wanted to see me about."

"The primary reason we're in Pittsburgh right now," Danny got right to it, "is for Mildred Matthison's funeral. Two of our best friends in the Grand Traverse area of Northern Michigan came with us so that we could honor and celebrate Mildred's life and service to Christ's Church at the funeral yesterday."

"Yes, I heard about that tragic accident, of course," Dennis looked slightly pained as he mentioned it. "I couldn't be there myself, but the presbytery sent our condolences to the congregation and Ms. Matthison's family. I don't really know what family members she still had. It was good of you to make the trip. I know the two of you worked well together for several years, and you have my sympathy and prayers also."

"Thank you, Dennis, we appreciate that. But I really wanted to ask you about something else regarding South Presbyterian Church. I'll preface my question with the frank admission that what I'm asking is absolutely none of my business, so you have no obligation to tell me anything. For that matter, if my asking seems over the line, I apologize in advance."

"Come on, Danny," Dennis immediately tried to put him at ease. "You can ask me anything. You and I go way back, and you have my trust."

"Thank you again. I'll get right to it in respect for your limited time. Just after the post-funeral luncheon at the church yesterday afternoon, I know there was a meeting in the church library with Pastor Tim Murphy and some key elders and leaders of the congregation. It appeared to be led by Todd Hickman, who I understand is now Chair of Property and Finance for Pittsburgh Presbytery. I have a particular and important reason for asking. If you feel able to tell me. I wonder what that meeting was about." Danny interrupted himself to hasten to add, "And again, I'm just the former pastor, and it's really none of my business. I refrained from asking Tim about it because I didn't want him to think that the old pastor was meddling in his church's business. I'm asking you confidentially."

Dennis leaned back in his chair and looked serious before answering.

"You're right, Danny. It is none of your business, but if the two of you promise to keep it to yourselves, I'll tell you. You're the honored Pastor Emeritus of South Presbyterian, so I'll break with my usual protocol and give you a little context. But what I'm about to say has not been disseminated to the congregation in general of your old church. And we really don't want any leak until it's the right and appropriate time to make an announcement. Are you okay with that?"

Danny and Andrea were practically on the edge of their chairs, wondering what it was that Dennis was about to tell them. Danny nodded, "We'll be discreet and keep whatever you can share to ourselves."

"I know you will. Right to the point, the buildings and grounds, all the property, of South Presbyterian Church is going to be sold, and the congregation dissolved."

Danny felt stunned, and Andrea knew that the statement hit him hard.

"Well, ah, well, I must admit that I'm taken by surprise. I mean, I knew that the membership had declined considerably, and that the giving and other income of the church had to be reduced as a result. But the new directions of inclusivity and More Light and expanded mission to the community seemed to offer new hope and vibrancy for the congregation. And what about Tim Murphy? It must be hard on him. He only arrived back at the church to be its new pastor over a year ago."

"You would be one of the relatively few to know this when I tell you. Tim was called by the congregation to be their pastor, yes, but leadership here on the presbytery level quietly charged him with preparing to dissolve the congregation and to ready the church to be sold. He's done an excellent job with that charge, and fully accepts the necessity of the move."

There was a moment of awkward silence before Dennis continued.

"I can see that this revelation is difficult for you to hear. One of the reasons I decided to fill you in on what's happening down there is out of appreciation for your ministry with South and in this presbytery in the past. Better that you hear it from me than through a grapevine of uninformed and disgruntled church members. Bottom line, and I apologize for the too-business-like term, the congregation was running annual deficits. It was becoming increasingly hard for them to maintain, repair, and in general keep things going. The surrounding neighborhoods were changing and becoming less 'oriented,' if you will, to Presbyterian-type churches. And though a difficult decision, as they always are, this direction is really for the best."

"And what about those new directions and programming and mission efforts and more inclusive membership?" Danny couldn't help himself to keep from asking. "Surely that wasn't just spinning the wheels and making a pretense? Why all that effort if the result was to close the church?"

Dennis shifted gears ever so slightly from being "pastoral" and explaining confidentially to a bit of a defensive posture. Danny hadn't meant to be accusatory, but the questions were reasonable.

"You know as well as I do, Daniel," Dennis spoke just slightly as though he was lecturing, "that so long as the church is there, ministry and mission still needs to be carried out in the name of Jesus Christ. What's been done under Tim's leadership has not been merely rearranging the deck chairs on the Titanic. Besides, part of the development plan for the property once it's sold is to convert the education building of the church into a new outreach center. The center would retain many of those mission emphases that are being introduced now. There just won't be a worshiping congregation there anymore, with a drafty old sanctuary that's expensive to heat, air condition, repair, maintain, clean and polish so that it looks pretty but stands empty most of the week. Now, if you can excuse me, it was great meeting you, Andrea. God's blessings on both of you and upon your retirement years, Danny."

Despite feeling rather abruptly dismissed with the shift in

tone of their discussion, Danny shook Dennis' hand and thanked him for his time and confidence.

"You're welcome. Please feel free to come back and visit in the future, but mum's the word on what I've told you, okay?"

"I understand completely," Danny assured him, "and thanks again."

As Andrea and he left Dennis' office and walked down the short hallway into the main office and reception area, Danny felt sure that he saw a man slip quickly out of the reception area and behind the closed door of the business manager's office. For the second consecutive day he thought he recognized the form of Todd Hickman.

"Didn't Dennis say that he was the only person in the office this morning?" Danny spoke softly to Andrea as they went out the door.

"He did, indeed," she agreed. "And I saw that man, too. And no one buzzed to be let in, nor did Dennis get up to let anyone in. Whoever it is, he had to have been there before we got there and during the whole time we were talking with Dennis."

* * *

After the Henriks left, Todd Hickman exited the office he had slipped into and went directly to Dennis' office.

"So, were they asking about our meeting yesterday in the church library?"

"They were indeed," Dennis confirmed. "That Danny Henriks is damnably compulsive about stirring things up and sticking his nose in where it doesn't belong. Long before I became General Minister – back when he and I were pastors here in the presbytery – he was frequently challenging decisions and actions that he didn't think were 'by the book,' or according to our set policies and standards."

"So, what did you tell him, Dennis?"

"Just what we agreed upon if he brought it up, that the congregation will be dissolved and most of the church buildings and property sold. And I pledged the two of them to secrecy, that I had only let him in on it out of respect and appreciation for his Pastor Emeritus status."

Todd looked concerned and a bit bothered. "And you think that he'll be satisfied with that 'inside information' and will let it go until they head home?"

"Well, I think it was better than trying to duck and cover and pretend that nothing was going on. He's good at putting the pieces together. Plus, he saw you meeting with those church leaders and Tim. Besides, they and their friends will be going back to Northern Michigan in a few days and re-entering their relaxing retirement. It's just a shame that the church secretary had to die like that, or they wouldn't have been here at all. And, he would have known nothing."

Todd grew even more serious and raised his voice somewhat. "Well, I hope he doesn't poke around any further like that secretary did. Or something will have to be done about him. There's too much at stake here, Denny." Todd left abruptly.

Dennis sighed, turned back toward his desk, and looked at the brass nameplate on the front of the desk: "The Rev. Dr. Dennis D. Lyons, General Minister." He thought of the cliché-like saying attributed to President Harry Truman so many years ago, that "the buck stops here." Why did he have to deal with Danny Henriks when things had been going so smoothly? And why did that church secretary have to die and complicate everything?

Well, nothing to do but stay calm and stay the course.

CHAPTER ELEVEN

The following day was Sunday, and the Henriks and the Joneses had agreed that they would go to worship at South Presbyterian. Frank Lewis had had a late night of activity with two different companions, and he slept in at his dingy room. He'd take a day off from shadowing the four visitors.

Although Danny didn't want to have any particular attention paid to his presence at the worship service, Tim had immediately spotted him. Actually, everyone there immediately spotted the giant Tiny and the gorgeous, model-like Angela as soon as they entered, and Danny and Andrea were with them. During announcement time after the initial musical prelude and welcome, Tim announced the attendance of "our beloved Pastor Emeritus" and his wife and friends, and there were smiles and applause throughout the congregation. Danny, Andrea, Tiny, and Angela were compelled to stand up and wave appreciatively.

The next announcement was on the part of the Clerk of Session, the top elected leader of the congregation, Alice Nelson, one of the people who attended the Friday afternoon meeting in the church library. Alice was very businesslike in her announcement.

"This is the second formal announcement of the congregational meeting that is called by the Session and will be held here in the sanctuary next Sunday morning immediately following the worship service. As stated previously, the sole purpose of this meeting will be to hear a report and recommendation from the Session and its Property and Finance Committee, and that will be the only business conducted. All members are asked to plan on attending and helping to establish a quorum. Thank you."

Andrea whispered to Danny in their back pew, "That seemed awfully terse. Isn't such an announcement usually a little more specific as to what the meeting is about?"

"I think that the key players here are holding their cards really close to their vests," Danny agreed. "If I were still here in this church, it would have been much more forthcoming to let people know what was being proposed. After the service, let's catch Alice Nelson and see if we can schedule a time to talk with her."

Following the benediction and during the postlude, Danny and Andrea approached Alice as her husband and she were standing near the front of the sanctuary.

"Dr. Henriks," Alice instantly beamed her well-practiced realtor's big smile and hearty handshake. "So glad that you folks were here for worship this morning."

"Thank you, Alice. It's good to be here. Although we're sorry that what brought us was Mildred's death and funeral Friday."

Alice immediately adopted a sorrowful scowl and responded with a "Yes, so sad. Terrible really." But she rallied in a flash and beamed the same smile with a slight flutter of her mascara-loaded eyelashes, "But thank you for coming over to say 'hi' to us."

"I wondered, Alice, if it would be convenient for us to stop by and see you in your office?" Danny asked.

"Of course," she beamed. "I'm showing houses for a client couple this afternoon, but will you still be here Monday morning. Say at 9:00?"

Danny looked at Andrea, and Tiny and Angela standing behind and replied, "I think 9:00 will be fine. Okay, guys?"

The other three nodded in the affirmative.

"Perhaps the Henriks and the Joneses are interested in buying here in the Pittsburgh area and moving back to get away from the bitter snow and cold of Northern Michigan?" Alice probed hopefully.

Danny cut her off gently, "We'll talk. Tomorrow morning at 9:00 in your office. Thank you."

* * *

Monday morning the Henriks and the Joneses left the William Penn shortly after 8:00 and drove in Tiny's Town Car to the real estate office of Alice Nelson in the South Hills area.

Frank Lewis watched them have breakfast in the first-floor restaurant at the hotel, and then he followed them at a distance in his Ford as they left the parking structure. When they went into Alice's office, he parked down the street and resumed reading the morning newspaper he had brought from the hotel.

Alice greeted her four guests as though they were about to be high-end clients. She gushed with even more enthusiasm than she had in church the day before, flashing her broadest smile and dazzling white teeth.

"I want you to know that I have cleared my schedule for you this morning. And, as soon as you provide me with your dreams for a new house in this Pittsburgh area, I can put you inside that dream for a close-up look."

Danny quickly pulled in her reins.

"As much as I admire your dedication to your work, Alice, Andrea and I are very happy with our home and its location east of Traverse City, Michigan."

Tiny couldn't resist joining the conversation.

"And Angela and I are likewise completely satisfied with our home in Suttons Bay, just north of Traverse City. Although I do still own some properties in the Hill District - Bedford Terrace and elsewhere," he added with exaggerated signs of pride. "Perhaps you could list them for me?"

As polished and professional as Alice was, she reflexively showed a slight grimace of disgust at Tiny's invitation. She ignored it as though she hadn't really heard him. Which would have been impossible as he raised his booming voice. She moved on.

"To what, then, do I owe the honor of this visit?" she asked, still smiling as though it had been frozen on her face. She glanced quickly at her open appointment book and daily calendar as though she was wondering what she could instantly restore to her plans for the morning.

Danny got right to the point. "Your announcement at worship yesterday morning. Next Sunday you and your Property and Finance Committee plan to recommend to the congregation that it be dissolved and the main church building and most of the property be sold, right?"

Alice had many years of professional and personal experience when it came to keeping her cards close to *her* vest, dodging questions and deflecting concerns voiced by others, but the directness of Danny's question caused just a hint of a hesitation.

Tim Murphy let me know yesterday at church that the Henriks had visited Dennis Lyons Saturday morning at the presbytery office, but I wasn't filled in on the entire content of that meeting. For all I knew, it was a social visit, she thought. *Damn church officials. Why can't they keep me in the loop so that I'm not blindsided like this?*

Alice had many years of experience with pastors and

presbytery staff members acting like the whole church scene was just another "good old boys club," or a lineup at the urinals in the men's room. Women stay in their secondary places and roles. Well, without her, this project wasn't going to stand a snowball's chance in anybody's image of hell. She knew well from all those years of experience that directness should be met with similar directness so as not to heighten suspicions.

"You're absolutely right, Dr. Henriks. As our esteemed Pastor Emeritus, I'm glad you've been kept informed as to the necessary future of South Presbyterian Church."

Andrea had kept silent as the initial conversation had taken place, but she could feel her own hackles rising as the phoniness and smugness of this woman. Alice's phrase of "necessary future" ignited a reaction that she instantly regretted.

"You mean, as in 'necessary death.'"

Another surprise confrontation made Alice feel at least a bit defensive, although she skillfully repressed her own desire to fire back.

"I mean as in the fact that all living things have life spans, even worshiping congregations. Every church is born at some point in history, lives and thrives, grows old, dwindles, and eventually dies. It's God's creative Design. The time has come for South Presbyterian to be put to rest with an appropriate celebration of all that it contributed for so many years," Alice rallied and reasserted her coolness and control. "And of course, that celebration is highlighted by your years of pastoral leadership and devoted service, Dr. Henriks." The plastered-on smile had been reset.

What Alice had said, Danny knew, was perfectly true. Even if the flattery was meant to back them off. *She's tough,* he thought as he listened to her mini lecture about church life spans. *We're not going to get anywhere unless I can get under her thick skin.*

"Assuming the congregation votes to accept the recommendation of your committee, and with Hickman's involvement, I would also assume that Pittsburgh Presbytery is on board. Would you be the listing agency for the impending sale?"

Alice immediately felt more defensive and resented his question and its implication, but she managed to maintain composure for the most part.

"Ah, well, yes, with my long relationship with South Hills Presbyterian and my many years of experience in real estate in that area, I guess it was natural that they would all look to me to provide the expertise to accomplish this job."

Bolstered by an occasional glance in her direction and bit of a frown from Andrea, Angela had also felt greatly put off by Alice's phoniness and posturing. She jumped into the discussion.

"I'm so sorry. You'll have to forgive me 'cause my background is inner-city Baptist, not Presbyterian until more recent years. But it seems like becoming the listing agent would be something of a conflict of interest, wouldn't it? Kinda like the professional photographer back in my old home church who was always insisting that the church use him to produce its pictorial directory. And then he could make money selling photo packages to his fellow church members."

Alice's façade crumbled around the edges. She couldn't help but exhibit some resentment and even anger that she had been put on the spot like this. Her response became somewhat more aggressive.

"It's no conflict of interest when all the involved parties are coming to me and requesting my expert help. And I'll have you know that I've offered to donate a large portion of the commission I would be due to the new mission center that is part of the proposal."

"Minus necessary expenses, government fees and permits, perhaps travel and other costs on your part?" Tiny added from his own business experience.

"I'm generous, Mr. Jones, but I can't afford to run my agency as a charity. You can well appreciate that I have my own overhead and cash flow challenges. You should know that the real estate business often involves months, even years, of out-go before any income is produced to recoup those expenses. My bills don't get paid until *I* get paid," Alice asserted with a hard edge of irritation in her tone.

She re-established her cool composure, reset her well-polished smile, although not as broadly as before, and moved to conclude this waste of her valuable time. "Thank you so much for coming to see me, all of you. I really must get on with the business of the day."

"Business of the day?" Danny smiled wryly to himself. *Whatever happened to "I've cleared my schedule for you?"* "We understand completely," he assured her. "We'll see ourselves out so that you can get right to it."

How much do they really know? Alice wondered as she watched them leave. *First that meddling church secretary, now the former pastor putting me on the spot. I can't afford to have him and his "entourage" messing around in this project. There's too much at stake.*

CHAPTER TWELVE

The two couples vigorously discussed their meeting with Alice once they were back in the car. Andrea and Angela were particularly heated.

"I couldn't stand that woman," Angela almost exploded. "She was so phony, so smug, so...so...so condescending and uppity."

"I know," Andrea agreed. "Don't care how many years of experience and how slickly 'professional' someone like that is, don't they know how people can see right through that falseness? Doesn't she ever look in a mirror and see the witch behind the mask?"

"My dear," Danny spoke up when the two had taken a breath, "I can assure you that for an astounding number of people that façade works. They somehow can't see beyond the superficial surface, the style and not the substance."

Tiny laughed and teased him as he drove them along. "You're sounding like some sort of cliché there, brother. 'Style, not substance.'"

"I know," Danny laughed at himself, "but it's true. An awful lot of the big-church pastors I've known over the years have their 'assets' or 'tickets' for their positions – usually tall, good-looking, terrific speaking voice, authoritative demeanor, articulate and socially adept."

"Socially manipulative might be another term," Andrea interrupted.

"Yes, fine line there between being skilled in social settings and simply being a master manipulator, telling people what they want to hear or what is apt to impress. But what I was going to say is that for some reason a lot of people are wowed and awed by that polished surface and style. I remember a woman who came to my congregation years ago who traveled many miles to be able to worship in a particular church because she adored the pastor. He was tall, clear baritone, folksy enough to make one gag. And she commented about what good friends they were. Well, one day I happened to mention to this guy that I had met this woman, and what devotion she had to drive so far to hear him preach. He practically knocked me over when he replied, 'Oh, yes, I know who you're talking about. She and I were never at all close,' he said dismissively as he turned to greet the next people standing there as though they were lifelong friends."

Andrea could tell when Danny was off on another verbal rambling, so she moved to bring the conversation back to Alice.

"Well, her phony posturing is one thing, but what we really learned, speaking of substance, is that she stands to be involved in a big real estate deal with the selling of the main church building and most of the property there. I would think there are numerous acres of valuable real estate there. Am I right?"

Angela did not want to let go of the subject of Alice's duplicity. "And she didn't convince me of her professed generosity in saying that she would donate a substantial part of her commission to the new mission and outreach center to be formed. Wouldn't that development be a pretty minor portion of the land at stake there? What about the rest of it, and the bulk of the buildings – the sanctuary, the offices, the youth center, the outbuildings? What happens to all that?"

"I think you just hit on the magic word in all of this, Ang" Danny leaned forward and spoke with more energy.

"Which word?" the other three responded practically in unison.

"Development," Danny replied forcefully. "Turn the car around, Tiny. I want to go back to that apartment building across the street from the church. I noticed there's a sign on the building by one of the doors that says 'Office.' I bet they can tell me what development and construction company built that building and undoubtedly the condo units alongside."

* * *

The four didn't know it, but when Tiny did a turn-around in a convenience store parking lot and headed toward the church, they passed an old Ford with Frank Lewis behind the wheel.

What's happening? Frank wondered. *Did they forget something?* He did the same drive through the convenience store parking lot and resumed following them. But he kept a good distance and made sure that at least two or three cars were between him and them. It was another useful skill that had gotten honed to professional status while he was incarcerated. How to tail someone in traffic and remain almost certain of being undetected.

Following the Henriks and the Joneses in their drives around the Greater Pittsburgh area was not a great source of enjoyment for Frank. Especially boring were the times he was forced to sit and do almost nothing while they were somewhere, like meeting with Alice. But he had developed a tremendous amount of patience and tolerance for being alone while he had been in prison. Truth be known, his own mind was his primary habitat after all those years, including the ones when he put himself into solitary confinement.

He had developed a strong appreciation for the fact that a high percentage of long-term prisoners found reentry into society at large genuinely difficult, if not virtually impossible. Their world had simply become too small, and they found psychological security in the structure, the security, the system of the prison. Their meals were provided. Their health needs were taken care of. They had social networks, however negative and unhealthy many of them were. The decisions they had to make in their daily lives were limited and simplified. One of the biggest facts that existed in the smaller and less complicated world of the prison was that their lives were uncluttered by a mass of things. Possessions. "Stuff" that filled so many lives on the outside. Frank had become very comfortable in his limited need and appetite for "stuff." And now he had a sizable amount of cash for anything he needed. Or wanted.

In any case, this practice in the art of tailing someone was temporary. Tremendously less demanding than the years of prison confinement. He didn't know what his anticipated opportunity would be. But he knew it would come. And he would recognize it when it did. For now, following and waiting was no big deal.

CHAPTER THIRTEEN

Danny had been right. He didn't even have to ask questions that would result in curiosity on the part of the apartment manager. A brochure in a small holder on the counter identified the apartment building as "...a property of the Steel City Development & Design Corporation, construction by Three Rivers Contractors." He told the manager that he merely wanted to pick up a brochure but may return later.

"Just give a call if you'd like to see an empty unit," the manager called after him as Danny went out the door.

Back in the car, Danny shared the brochure with Tiny, Angela, and Andrea.

"This is just a hunch on my part," he admitted, "but I seriously wonder if Steel City Development and Design and/or Three Rivers Contractors have any direct connections to South Hills Presbyterian Church."

"You don't mean that you think the planned demise of the church is part of an insidious development scheme, do you?" Andrea asked skeptically. "Would outfits like those *really* try to destroy a long-established church?"

"Believe me," Danny insisted, "it's been done in other places before."

"Damn right," Tiny said. "If the mayor of Pittsburgh and

his cronies could scheme to kick hundreds and hundreds of Hill District residents out of their homes and apartments to do their highly profitable development, a move like this one pales in comparison. 'They'll just have to go somewhere else,' the bastard said to Danny, me and all the others in that meeting." Tiny still fumed when he thought of that chaotic day so many years ago now.

"Besides, in what other direction can they go?" Danny asked rhetorically, "the hillside opposite the church was the last open area nearby, and it's all built up now. But in a developer's hungry eyes South Presbyterian has acres just aching to be filled with construction. *If* they can get rid of the congregation. And the main church buildings."

"What should we do at this point?" Angela asked, feeling agitated herself with thoughts of what Danny and Tiny were saying.

Just then Danny's cell phone rang. It was an unfamiliar number, but he decided to interrupt their discussion to see who it was.

"Jenny, what a pleasant surprise. How are you today? Good, good. But you sound a bit concerned." Danny listened as Jenny explained her reason for calling. "Sure, I can stop by and see you there. What time?... Okay, it's a date.... No, Andrea won't think we're dating, you flirt," he kidded.

"That was Jenny Kennedy," Danny explained to the other three. "She got my cell phone number from Tim Murphy. She said that with the busyness of Mildred's funeral last Friday she forgot all about it. 'Senior moment,' she laughed, but that she had something for me from Mildred. Apparently, something Mildred gave her, but she didn't know what to do with it. Anyway, her Dorcas Circle of older ladies is meeting at the church tomorrow morning for their monthly meeting, and she wondered if I could stop by, and she would pass it on to me."

"I can drive you there again if you want," Tiny offered.

"No, we've been chewing up a lot of time on my 'itch scratching' about Mildred's death and what's going on at my old church. Why don't you plan on doing some more of your showing Angela around the Greater Pittsburgh area? I can take the rental car over to the church to see Jenny for a little bit. Besides, depending on what else we find out today, I may just want to pop in on Tim again. If he's in the office. Andrea, you might want to take a break from this craziness of mine and tour around with Tiny and Angela while I do that," he suggested.

"Sounds good to me," she agreed. "But under the condition that you don't get yourself into another situation that involves some 'crazy' gunning for my husband."

"I'll be good," Danny assured her. "How dangerous can it be meeting with a little old widow lady like Jenny?"

"I don't know, man," Tiny acted overly worried. "Our history together shows that while I'm a chick magnet...ah, used to be, that is. Not since I met Angela." Angela whacked his massive arm and scowled at him. Tiny cringed with an exaggerated expression of pain and continued, "You, on the other hand, have seemed to be a beacon for femmes fatales, women scorned, and black widows."

"He has a point, Daniel," Andrea piled on Tiny's ribbing of Danny. "Maybe sweet, little old Jenny had a murderous grudge against Mildred, who stole her secret recipe for apple pie."

Danny loved apple pie, especially made from the Northern Spy apples that would soon be ripening in Northern Michigan orchards. "Well, while I wouldn't condone murder under any circumstances..." He made a pretense of thinking hard and long. "At least if it was over a great, secret apple pie recipe it would be more understandable. Not justifiable, but understandable."

All four of them laughed and nodded at that comment. They knew all-too-well about Danny's love for pie. Especially his spring favorite, rhubarb, the raspberry pies of summer, and mouth-watering fresh apple pie in the fall...and pumpkin...and mince...and, well, it was hard to come up with a pie that Danny didn't love.

"Well, we have a plan for Tuesday morning," Andrea grew serious again. "But what about Angela's question? What should we do now with what we learned so far? You obviously think that Steel City Development and Design and their building contractors are involved somehow in the closing of the church."

"I admit," Danny answered, "that it's all speculation and uncertainty at this point. And maybe a part of me deep down inside is just upset about the prospects of my old congregation closing its doors. But it just doesn't seem to me that the church is so precarious that it would have to fold. I must wonder if *somebody* has a big-time desire to get rid of South Presbyterian." Danny checked the time before continuing.

"There's a fine little Italian pizza and sub shop not far from here. Why don't we grab a little lunch, do some research online? And then before we drive down to the Mt. Washington area for some more sightseeing, would you mind if we dropped in at the home office of Steel City Development and Design? I'd like to know a bit more about what projects they may have in the works."

"I think all three of us are in agreement with that idea," Andrea responded as Tiny and Angela nodded affirmatively. "And an Italian veggie wrap sounds good to me."

"I'm ready for a large pepperoni pizza myself," Tiny licked his lips.

"Sorry, big boy," Angela brought him up short. "You know what your doctor said last visit. You're a long way from your hours of football practice, running laps and lifting weights every day. I have a strange desire to keep you around to treat me like I deserve in our retirement. So, like it or not, you're going to watch your girlish waistline. You can split a pizza with me. And you're not poaching more than half for yourself."

"Half a pizza?" Tiny wailed in protest. "How can I pamper you while traveling around the world if you've starved me to death before we even get under way? You're like a prison warden, woman."

"Well, if I really was one, I could probably control your diet a lot better," Angela fired back. "You can thank the Good Lord in heaven that I'm not force-feeding you nothing but salad and tofu."

"Tofu?" Danny questioned. "I've never seen Big Tiny eat tofu."

"That's because he'd rather have large pepperoni pizzas, sometimes two at a time," Angela huffed. "But we're going to have much less 'Big' and much more 'Tiny' around here if I have anything to say about it. And I do," she concluded forcefully, glaring at him behind the wheel.

It always amused Danny that when in the direct path of one of Angela's "stormy outbursts," his giant friend would physically hunker down and wait for it to pass. He chuckled quietly to himself as Big Tiny truly looked smaller at that moment, his broad shoulders hunched in slightly and his head drawn down turtle-like. His chuckle continued and became audible at the pizza and sub shop as his best friend ordered an Italian salad for himself instead of the pizza. Danny appreciated fully what it was like to love a strong woman who loved so fiercely in return.

CHAPTER FOURTEEN

Frank pulled over to the curb well ahead of Tiny's Town Car near the pizza shop. There had been a spot open just two spaces behind their car, but Frank knew enough about tailing that he didn't want Tiny or any of the others to be able to look into a rear-view mirror and see the same old blue Ford that had been driving behind them in traffic. He went into a coffee shop down the street from the pizzeria and sat near a window where he could keep watch for when they came out again.

I really would like to catch his holiness, the Rev. Doctor, alone for what I have in mind, Frank thought, *but he's always with his wife and the big guy and his wife. After today, I only have Tuesday and Wednesday to confront him. Then they'll be off back to Michigan on Thursday. I sure as hell don't want to tussle with Danny and Tiny again back there. That did not turn out well for me the first time. Besides, Pittsburgh is really my home turf. At least it was until I stabbed the old bastard and took his money.*

Frank started to slip down the old, slimy slope of stewing about how everyone in his lifetime had conspired to destroy him and abused him along the way to his destruction. His parents, his professors in college and seminary, his bishop, his rector, Bill Brand, his lover, Sarah Brand, and finally her old lover, Daniel Henriks. And then there was his good-for-nothing shark of an attorney at his trial, the bloodthirsty prosecutor, the self-deified judge, the jury that wanted to find him guilty as quickly as possible and get back to their daily soap operas. Followed by the warden, his demonic guards, the scurvy lot of prison inmates. Every damn person who ever came into his life had added a tortuous turn to the wheel of the rack that tore him apart so unjustly and painfully.

But the real focal point was Henriks. *I managed to struggle through all that shit that was heaped upon me until he messed with Sarah and forced me to try to get rid of him so that she and I could find happiness together.*

But Devil calmed down as he watched the pizza shop and continued his vigil. *No,* the controlled and disciplined Frank capped his caldera of hate and violence once again, *I cannot let my righteous rage distort my purpose here. My thoughts and decisions must be clear, cool, and well-calculated. I will not be rushed. I will not become rash. I will not risk jeopardizing the right time to act. I will prevail.*

* * *

Tiny munched on his Italian salad and uttered murmurs of "m-m-m, good" with an enthusiasm that did not seem like him. Angela sat next to him, enjoying her salad wrap, the same order that Andrea had gone for, and smiled approvingly at Tiny's munching. Danny and Andrea sat across from them and as they ate their lunch, they searched for the Steel City Development and Design website on Andrea's laptop.

"Okay," Andrea said as she clicked on various links the website offered. "Here's one that provides descriptions of current or recent projects that Steel City Development is involved in. Luxury condos in Sewickley and Fox Chapel, a planned community down in the Mt. Washington area. Don't see anything about plans for a development in the South Hills."

"Well, they probably wouldn't post anything yet when they don't even have the land secured. If I'm right, they have their sights fixed on South Presbyterian Church. And its acres. Try that one that says, 'Our Leadership Team.'"

"Okay, we have photos and profiles of the top corporate officers – CEO, Chief Operating Officer, Head Designer..."

"There," Danny interrupted her, "click on Chief Financial Officer. And look at that smiling face. It's none other than the unknown man I saw sitting at the table in the church library last Saturday. I assumed that he must have been a newer church member who had joined after I left the pastorate. But he was actually representing Steel City Development. Now why would Alan Alderman, CFO, bother to go to a Friday afternoon meeting at the church?"

"And look," Andrea added. "Look at who is a Board of Directors member."

"Hey, you two," Danny said to Tiny and Angela across from him, "I think we've got something here."

Tiny wiped a spot of ranch dressing from the corner of his mouth, indulging in the smallest hint of displeasure as he did so, and looked up. Angela swallowed a bit of her wrap sandwich.

"Remember I told you about the, well, I would now call it 'mysterious,' meeting I saw going on in the church library right after Mildred's post-funeral luncheon? There must have been some urgent and compelling reasons for that meeting. Especially given the roles of those present. Pastor Tim was there, of course. And Alice Nelson, who is the Clerk of Session and top elected officer of the congregation, and also happens to be the realtor who would be listing the sale of the church and its property. Bernie Recker, a senior elder on the Session who has a lot of influence among the church membership. This Alan Alderman who is the Chief Financial Officer of Steel City Development. And moderating the meeting, Todd Hickman, who is now the Chair of the Property and Finance Committee of Pittsburgh Presbytery."

"Now I've been an active Presbyterian for a lot of years," Andrea added, "and I can tell you that not only is that a lot of ecclesiastical firepower to gather in the library of South Presbyterian Church. But on a Friday afternoon? Hickman and Alderman should have been off playing golf, maybe even in a foursome together the way this is looking. Alice should have been showing clients around her choice listings. And after having so much of the end of his week taken up with Mildred's death arrangements, you would think that poor Tim Murphy would want to be finishing up his sermon for last Sunday."

"Well, it sure looks like a power broker meeting to me," Tiny concluded dabbing the corner of his mouth with a napkin after Angela had pointed to it. "And why would this Alderman fellow be there unless his company had a large, vested interest in what happens to the church?"

"Precisely," Danny grew more intense. "And why would Hickman be there unless it was something big that needed presbytery input and approval? I think that the dots are connecting. And that the presbytery is backing the closing of the church so that it can be sold to Steel City Development. Probably for more condos, or fancy apartments. And Alice Nelson is not only the listing real estate broker facilitating the sale, but she also stands to make a huge commission in the deal. Despite her claims that she would donate 'a large portion' of the commission due her to the proposed, new mission and outreach center."

"And as frosting on the Nelson cake," Andrea jumped in,

"guess who's a key member of the Board of Directors of Steel City Development?" She eagerly rushed to answer her own question without bothering to wait for guesses. "Nathaniel Nelson, who happens to be Alice's 'ex.'"

"As her ex-husband, wouldn't it perhaps be more likely that he would be uncooperative in any project that Alice was involved in?" Angela asked. "You know, 'Damned if I'm going to help you reap some big commission on one of our developments.'"

"Ah, but I remember that divorce," Danny said. "it occurred while I was the pastor. It was one of those divorces that we refer to as 'amicable.' Now 'amicable' is often a public veneer for a broken relationship where a lot of hurt and unhappiness is covered over for appearances sake. But Alice and Nate really did part on friendly terms. In fact, both the forging of the marriage in the beginning and its dissolution at the end reminded one more of a mutually agreeable business deal than a matter of love and passion."

"Their several years together were characterized by Alice always being off showing properties and meeting with clients 24/7. At least it would have been '24' if she could have gotten people to go with her in the middle of the night. And Nate wheeling and dealing and schmoozing big development 'angels' at all the top country clubs in Western Pennsylvania. If we dug into the post-divorce history of the two, I wouldn't be surprised if we found that they've been colluding on real estate sales and development proposals in several instances since they broke up. Unencumbered by the necessities of sharing domestic life together."

"Shoot, given what we saw of her this morning," Tiny grinned a bit grimly, "I wouldn't be surprised if they were still doing the horizontal mambo, too, if they could fit it into their schedules."

"And if it would help stimulate the deal," Andrea added.

"Oo-o, girl, you're being nasty," Angela chided her laughingly.

"So, if in fact these dots are connecting," Tiny directed his question back toward Danny, "what would you guess about Tim Murphy and Bernie Recker and their roles in this scheme to shut the doors of South Presbyterian Church?"

"I've mentally scratched my head about what Bernie's involvement might be. I initially thought he might just be a key Session member participating. You know, so that the elders of the church could be represented in this ad hoc task force meeting. Or whatever it might be called. But then it also occurred to me that Bernie used to talk from time to time about his love of investing. He made good money as the owner of a small chain of gas stations and convenience stores."

"Damn right he would have made money, not that I'd call it 'good,' at the prices those places charge for gas at the pump and a 'convenient' loaf of bread and jug of milk," Angela groused.

"Well, even more likely on the profits for all those cases of beer, chips, beef jerky, and gooey donuts," Danny took back his line of discussion. "But back to Bernie, I frankly wouldn't be surprised if he had the financial reserves to be able to be one of those investment 'angels' for Nate Nelson and Steel City Development. In fact, yet another one of his stores might be part of the development plan. If the zoning allows for it."

"Hell," Tiny interjected, "even if zoning doesn't allow it. With the big money all those players represent, they can get their legal lackeys working and greasing palms under the table to get zoning changed, or exemptions issued. Or hell, just about any kind of 'looking the other way.'"

"And as far as Tim is concerned," Danny finally concluded his answer, "the fact that he wasn't moderating a meeting of elders in his own church is an indication, to me, that while he had to be included as a key person in the planned future of the congregation..."

"Or lack of future, to be more accurate," Andrea tossed in.

"Right," Danny acceded. "As pastor, Tim had to be included. But he's probably being pushed aside and feels run over by all this. I feel bad for him. His first spouse shot to death right after their wedding at South Presbyterian Church. Two times he's been asked to minister to that congregation and both times it's ended badly. Especially with the closing of the church so soon after he became pastor. And with his church secretary dying in a tragic incident just over a week ago. That's horrible enough if it had been an accident. But much worse if I'm right, and it was murder. I don't know how he's holding up during all this."

"Well, didn't you tell us that when you met with Dennis Lyons, the General Presbyter, last Saturday that he said that Tim had been charged with preparing the church to be closed and the congregation dissolved," Tiny reminded him. "So, he must have been expecting all that to be happening, and had agreed to facilitate it, you said."

"That's true," Danny ceded, "but the way Dennis said it to me, I have the strong impression that Tim didn't know that was in the ecclesiastical cards when he accepted the call to return to the church to become their new pastor. I think that he undoubtedly got blindsided once he arrived, felt that he had no choice in the matter, and went along to be a faithful Presbyterian and a good 'soldier' for Christ. Follow orders and do what seemed necessary for the good of the entire Body. Which would have made the tragedies of all this even more painful and disappointing for him."

Andrea added, "And he probably doesn't have anywhere to turn for his own support and help. The presbytery seems all too eager to 'throw him under the bus.' He has the most powerful elders in his congregation who probably don't give a rat's ass what happens to him so long as they make their big bucks in this sale and development. There are overwhelming corporate interests whose concern for a struggling church and its pastor has about the longevity of a snowball in hell."

"Well, I'm sure he has the love and support of his new spouse, Jeremy," Danny suggested, "but I'm going to offer him mine, too. I'll be at the church tomorrow to meet Jenny and get what she has for me from Mildred. I'm sure Tim will be there in his study in the morning after his usual Monday day off. I'll sit down and have a little heart-to-heart with him if he's open to that. And, if he's willing to disclose what's really going on, of course. Besides, there are at least two big, unanswered questions that I'd like to see if he could shed some light on. If I can get him to talk."

"Which are?" Andrea pressed him.

"What was the urgent reason for that unusual meeting last Friday in the church library? We still don't have any idea why they 'exposed' themselves like that for a casual observer like me to walk by and notice their gathering."

"And the other?" Andrea prompted.

"The biggest one. What really happened to Mildred? Was it murder? If so, why? Even though we haven't seen any connection whatsoever, could it be related to the sale and closure of the church? Or did last Friday's meeting have nothing whatsoever to do with Mildred's demise? Was it strictly coincidental?"

"Now, the three of us know that you don't believe in coincidences," Angela countered him.

"I don't," Danny admitted. "At the risk of being too theological and cosmological, I don't believe that God has random events taking place with no connection to each other. I believe that everyone and everything in the universe is connected. Very often in ways beyond our ability to perceive or understand. And I believe in cause and effect. Events happen for reasons that compel them to take place. And somehow, I don't think that Mildred's funeral was just a remarkably convenient and coincidental time for those movers and shakers to get together and talk new construction plans. 'Oh, there's somebody's funeral at the church. What a good time to have a meeting afterwards.'"

Danny made eye contact with each of his companions before continuing.

"Think of it this way. Those principal players in the 'close the church and sell it off for development' drama would surely have detailed plans and preparations all in place by now to have a meeting of the congregation called for next Sunday to vote on the whole idea. And it would have been worked out behind closed doors in private, even secret settings and sessions well before last Friday. What would have been the reason for what seems increasingly like a hastily-put-together meeting right there? In plain view? In the church library? Maybe Mildred's death, and her funeral, somehow affected the whole scheme, and introduced a new complication that must be dealt with."

"I know, I know," Danny backed away from the table but continued. "I get these obsessions and compulsively ride them when it seems like nobody else sees a valid reason to climb on. I guess I just can't help myself. But you three must agree. I've been right before. At least some of the time."

"You have, love. You have." Andrea leaned closer and put her arm around him tenderly.

"And we're with you, bro'" Tiny reached across and put a giant hand on his other shoulder. "We'll figure it all out." Angela nodded and smiled, encouraging one of her best friends in the whole world.

"Well then," Danny enthusiastically smiled and shifted

gears, "you won't mind finishing up those lunches and we'll get going to the headquarters of Steel City Development and Design. Even if there's nothing on this website about a new development planned for the site of South Presbyterian Church, there must be at least a few of their people who can confirm the existence of such proposals and plans. We just need someone to relax and 'spill the beans' on the drafting board to confirm what we're thinking. Otherwise, it's just our speculation at this point."

Tiny pushed what remained of his salad toward the center of the table. "You know, that was just so filling. I'm done. Let's get going." Angela shook her head. She was going to have to keep an eye on him for the rest of the afternoon, so that his big mitts didn't sweep up candy bars wherever they went.

I better even make sure that he doesn't wander into whatever break room they have at Steel City Development, or they could be out all their bagels and muffins in a flash.

CHAPTER FIFTEEN

On the way to Steel City Development and Design corporate headquarters in Monroeville, the four discussed a strategy for digging out some confirmation of a planned development for the site of South Presbyterian Church.

"Tiny, you're the successful businessman here. You know what those dynamics are like," Danny argued. "You're driving up to the gate of their parking lot in a new Lincoln Town Car. I think you're the one to go in and see if you can peel back the layers of secrecy regarding South Presbyterian."

"Besides," Andrea pointed out, "We can't risk that someone in there might recognize Daniel from his years as the pastor of the congregation. They surely know the recent history of the church and the people they would have to deal with."

"Or dispose of," Danny remarked wryly. "Let Andrea and me off up ahead there at the Starbucks, and Angela and you go on to the corporate offices and give it your best shot. Not only do I trust Angela's instincts and perceptions in situations like this, but she's such a head-turner that you'll be able to paw through a guy's file cabinet and copy off proposals without him even noticing that you're there with her."

"Daniel Henriks," Angela protested with exaggerated indignation, "that is so-o sexist. I'm not along to be somebody's 'eye candy.' But once again, you're right," she smiled alluringly. "If Tiny can't get the answers he needs with his questions, I can have some draft board jockey begging for the chance to tell me more." She batted her beautiful eyes.

After dropping the Henriks off at the Starbucks, Tiny and Angela drove down the road and turned into the gated drive of Steel City Development and Design. A uniformed security guard spoke to them from a booth. The developers obviously took their corporate security very seriously.

Tiny rolled the driver's window down and spoke to the guard in a confident tone. "Good afternoon, brother. My wife and co-owner and I don't have an appointment. But we were told on the phone that if we drove over this afternoon, there would be someone in the Development Proposal Division who could sit down with us and have a preliminary discussion about designing a housing development on the acreage we have available in the South Pittsburgh area. Could you confirm for us that this is a possible time to meet with someone?"

The guard nodded, "Yes, sir." He picked up his phone, punched in an extension, and had a muffled conversation with someone.

"I'm afraid, sir, that all our senior proposal designers are tied up right now. But if you don't mind, we do have someone who could meet with you. They can find out the basics of what you have in mind, answer initial questions about the company and its history of development projects, and at least get a start on what we're sure would be a most satisfactory working relationship."

"Just what we had hoped. Thank you, brother," Tiny said as he reached out and slipped a fifty-dollar bill into the guard's hand.

"Oh, ah, sir, I really appreciate it, but we're not allowed to accept tips from clients or visitors."

"Our secret, young man. I used to work security myself, and I have a pretty good idea of what your wages are like. If nothing else, take your sweetie out for a nice meal, and maybe you can do a favor for me in return one of these days." Tiny didn't tell him, of course, that until quite recently he had been the hugely successful founder, owner, and CEO of "Tiny's Big Security Services and Investigations" in the Grand Traverse, Michigan area.

"I assume you had a reason for forcing that generous tip on the young man," Angela commented as they drove up to the main doors of the corporation and found a visitor's parking spot.

"I did indeed," Tiny smiled. "If for some reason, this doesn't play out well, and we're suspected to be spies by some paranoid corporate lackeys, we may just want a grateful ally who will raise the gate for our speedy getaway."

After checking in at the reception desk, Tiny and Angela sat in a comfortable waiting area furnished with upholstered club chairs, a genuine Persian rug, a coffee table with magazines that were current issues, and a flat screen mounted on the wall that was tuned with low volume to Fox News. Tiny looked unsuccessfully for a remote to change the channel, but while he was doing so, an attractive young blonde woman in a smart business suit came out and greeted them cordially.

"Mr. Jones, Mrs. Jones, I'm Samantha Dirk – please call me 'Sam,' and I'm on the Development Proposal Team here at Steel City Development and Design. I can have that initial consultation with you regarding your development needs and dreams. If you would, please follow me."

They did so as Samantha led them out of the reception

area, down a hallway and into a small conference room with a large, detailed map of the Greater Pittsburgh area. Angela and Tiny could readily see that past Steel City development projects were outlined in red, with lines connecting each one out to the large margins around the map, where photos and brief descriptions identified each of the developments.

"My preliminary information is that the two of you require plans and designs for the construction of a housing development on acreage that you own in the South Hills region of Pittsburgh?"

"Yes," Tiny confirmed. "It should be comprised of individual homes, condo units, and at least one luxury apartment building for high-end rentals."

Samantha smiled in anticipation of what sounded like a very profitable project.

"Let's start with location. Exactly where is your acreage? How many buildable acres are there? What occupies the land now? And we'll need to determine if sufficient infrastructure exists to support what you plan to have built, check zoning restrictions, of course..."

Tiny saw through Sam's thorough but over-done blizzard of questions. She was obviously an ambitious but somewhat inexperienced middle-level design professional.

"To answer your first question," he interrupted her as he got up from the conference table and walked over to the large map, "our property is right there." And he pointed to the exact spot in the South Hills occupied by the South Presbyterian Church.

Samantha stepped to his side, peered closely at the map where his big index finger was pointing, paused, consulted some papers clipped onto the clip board she was holding, looked again, and expressed some confusion.

"I'm sorry, Mr. Jones, but that location can't be right. Could you please check your location? Perhaps you missed your spot?"

"No, ma'am, I didn't miss. This is exactly where we need our development built. Is there a problem with that?" He sounded a bit indignant at being challenged.

Flustered by what she was looking at and his sudden belligerence, Samantha stammered and blurted, "Well, I'm sorry, but it appears that we already have a development project proposed for that same area. Are you absolutely sure you've pointed to the right spot?"

"Come on, dear," Tiny wheeled and addressed Angela as she rose from her seat. "It seems that Steel City Development has gotten ahead of us and presumes to build before we've even signed with them. Perhaps our attorneys should talk to yours, Sam."

The Joneses left the room, walked briskly down the hall in the direction from which they had come, and hustled past the reception desk toward the outer door.

Samantha felt confused and rattled by what had just happened, but she got on an inner-office extension as soon as Tiny and Angela departed and let her supervisor know about the incident. The senior management executive brushed aside her stammering excuses and apologies.

"You're sure that was the parcel they insisted they owned and wanted to have developed?"

"Yes, sir," Sam confirmed. "Mr. Jones was adamant that that was their acreage."

"Thank you," the executive spoke briskly, "we'll talk later," and he hung up the phone.

Poor Samantha was left shaking with apprehension about what she had done wrong and what might happen. The executive immediately phoned the outer guard booth and requested that a black Lincoln Town Car be stopped and held up from leaving.

"The Joneses left here with proprietary information, and

they cannot be allowed to leave before I'm down there to straighten it out."

The security guard waved smilingly at Tiny as he drove by and replied to the executive, "I'm really sorry, sir, but they've already gone by." *In four years of doing this crappy job,* the guard thought as he clicked off his phone, *that brother was the only one who ever gave me anything but grief and 'tude. Whatever they walked off with, it can be someone else's problem.*

The executive called CFO Alan Alderman and told him what had just happened. Alderman immediately called Director Nate Nelson. "We have a problem."

CHAPTER SIXTEEN

Tiny and Angela huddled with Danny and Andrea in the Starbucks and the Joneses reported on their adventure at Steel City Development and Design.

"You were right, Danny," Tiny admitted. "Since we didn't have an appointment, the only designer available to meet with us was a mid-level young woman who was full of enthusiasm and energy, but short on experience and savvy."

"I couldn't believe," Angela gushed, "how my sugar almost bullied her into blurting out that Steel City Development already had plans to build on the site of your old church, Danny."

"So that definitely confirms that realtor Alice Nelson, Alan Alderman and Steel City, and probably Todd Hickman of the presbytery are all colluding to take over South Presbyterian, tear it down, and build more luxury housing on the acreage," Andrea concluded. "But that's downright demonic. Destroying a fine church and its congregation just, just to..."

"Make money," Danny finished her statement for her, "and lots of it. Many millions. All the players in this scenario would probably not hesitate to sell off and demolish the Vatican itself if they had the ability to do it. None of those people are going to shed any tears for South Presbyterian and its people and ministries."

"But it makes me want to cry for people like Tim Murphy and Jeremy, Jenny Kennedy, and poor Mildred," Andrea said sadly. "It would be horrible if I knew that real estate wolves, cold-hearted developers, and big money people were conspiring to destroy our Presbyterian Church back in Traverse City. Oh, and South Presbyterian is your old church, Daniel. You must be pained about all this."

"Well, what really bothers me," he confessed, "is that as admittedly sad as all that is, the rampant greed that seems to be going on here may well be the motive to murder an elderly church secretary. And on the last day of work before she finally retired. We don't know the connection to Mildred in all this yet, but I feel stronger and stronger that there must be one."

"Well, with all that we've found out today," Tiny concluded, "I guess our planned sightseeing trip down to Mt. Washington this afternoon is postponed indefinitely."

"We *are* out here on the east edge of the Greater Pittsburgh area," Danny pointed out. "What say we finish up our lattes, take a bit of a break from all this investigating effort, and keep driving out to Ligonier, say visit old Fort Ligonier? I don't know about you, but I think I need to ruminate a bit on all this information and skullduggery."

"Sounds good to me," Andrea agreed, "and there are a lot of pastures and cows out there around Latrobe and Ligonier. So, it has to be a good place to 'ruminate,'" she snickered.

"Oh, that's just terribly corny," Danny protested, "making fun of me when I'm trying to figure out this mystery."

"He's right," Angela jumped on, "where there are cows there's invariably corn." She hooted as she dissolved into uncontrollable laughter.

Andrea was laughing so hard that she could barely get out her next words, "which is what you'd...you'd expect, digging into his skull. Corn, and, oh, God, more corn." She finally couldn't talk anymore.

The commotion caused all the baristas, the other customers, and a delivery guy to stop and look over at the table in the corner occupied by the Henriks and the Joneses, where the two women were laughing and crying and slapping the table, and a giant fellow had doubled over and almost fallen out of his chair and onto the floor with his guffaws and bellows. Danny was the only one not paralyzed with laughter, and he sat with his hands outspread, looked at the other people in the store, and shook his head.

"Sorry, folks. I guess it was something I said. We'll be sure to clean up after ourselves." *And I sure hope we can find a way to clean up the mess that we're uncovering with South Presbyterian and Mildred's death,* he thought grimly as the commotion began to calm down.

When it came to mysteries, Danny had to admit to himself his natural reserve and stuffiness, his penchant for neatness, order, and logic, and his compulsiveness to have things make sense. It was a wonder that the people who knew him best and loved him the most so often found him to be hilarious.

Are words like "ruminate" and "skullduggery" really that funny? He wondered. *A bit old-fashioned, I suppose, but perfectly good words, just the same. Well, even if it's sometimes at my expense, we sure have fun.*

Danny joined in the subsiding laughter. It's always good to laugh at yourself.

CHAPTER SEVENTEEN

Monday had been an incredibly long, busy, jam-packed day for Danny, Andrea, Tiny, and Angela. Starting with the tense meeting with Alice Nelson, the stop by the new luxury apartments across from South Presbyterian, the probing of Steel City Development and Design, Corp., and the sightseeing trip out to Fort Ligonier. It was well into the evening when they finally got back to the William Penn hotel and turned in for the night.

* * *

Frank Lewis had continued to follow them from a safe distance as Danny and Andrea had stopped off at the Starbucks while Tiny and Angela made their visit to Steel City Development. Frank figured that Danny and Andrea wouldn't leave each other's side while they took their coffee break. So, even though Danny was his real target, he decided to follow the Joneses to the development and design company.

He had become increasingly curious about just what the four of them were up to. And he had started to put together his own speculations about what was going on after the elimination of the church secretary.

I can't tell if they suspect foul play with the secretary's death or not. But, they seem to be focused on real estate and land development. I wonder if it has something to do with the church. If so, it's a good bet that the Rev. Dr. Henriks will be going back there tomorrow. Or Wednesday. Sometime before they plan to leave on Thursday, for sure. I must catch him alone. That's probably the place and opportunity to do it.

Frank followed Tiny and Angela back to the Starbucks. But when the four drove off South and east on Interstate 76 and U. S. 30 toward Latrobe and Ligonier, he broke off and headed back to his seedy downtown hotel. He had two more days, he figured, to accomplish his goal, and he would continue to be patient until the right time and place.

And what better place? If it turns out to be his precious, old church, I will prevail.

* * *

Andrea, Tiny and Angela all decided to sleep in after their exhausting Monday, figuring that they could go down together to the morning brunch before it ended at 10:00. Afterward, they would go in Tiny's Town Car back to his old Hill District again, where he had some cousins who wanted him to stop by. They would meet up with Danny later for a late lunch in Highland Park, not far from the Pittsburgh Theological Seminary.

Danny had gotten up a good deal earlier, careful not to awaken Andrea, had a continental breakfast at the coffee bar on the first floor of the hotel, and drove in his rental car down to South Presbyterian Church to meet Jenny Kennedy about ten minutes before her 9:00 a.m. meeting of the Dorcas Circle ladies.

He waited in the lounge just down the hall from the door

to the parking lot and rose when Jenny came in at 8:52.

"Please forgive me if I've kept you waiting, Dr. Henriks," Jenny apologized.

"Not at all, Jenny. I just got here myself."

A polite fiction, she thought. She remembered Danny well from when he was the pastor. He would have been there early. *The Good Lord didn't make servants any more conscientious than the Rev. Dr. Daniel Henriks.*

"I wish we could visit a spell and catch up on things," Jenny said with much sincerity, "but my Dorcas sisters await me, and I have opening devotionals today, so I hope you don't mind if I just give you this from Mildred and look forward to another time for us to be together."

She reached into her big, hand-woven Mexican tote bag and pulled out a small, white mailer envelope with a brass clasp that was glued shut. The outside of the envelope was written in ink with Mildred's hand, "Unholy Evidence."

Danny looked at it, turned it over and back. There were no other markings. He wrinkled his brow.

"Sounds rather ominous. You didn't open it and look inside, Jenny? Mildred entrusted it to you."

Jenny reacted with definite agitation. "Well, Mildred told me not to do so. She said that it was papers that she had gathered and had squirreled away in the back of her bottom desk drawer here at the church, and that it wasn't safe or wise for her to keep them at the church any longer. In fact, she said that she wanted them out of her possession entirely until they were needed before long. And that while she didn't want me involved by knowing too much, she knew she could entrust me to keep them safe. And Dr. Henriks, the next part has me just so upset, especially with that terrible accident that took Mildred's life. She said that it was best for someone else like me to keep them, 'just in case.' It's like she knew the Good Lord would take her at any time."

"And she didn't give you any idea of what was inside?"

Jenny shook her head and dabbed at a corner of her right eye with an embroidered hankie.

"One more thing, Jenny. If you don't mind my asking, why did you decide to give this to me?"

"Well, I just didn't know what to do, you see. Mildred said that I shouldn't open it. So, I took it home and put it in the center drawer of my antique drop-down writing desk. And I rather put it out of my mind, you know, waiting until she asked for it back. Then she died in the accident." Jenny's teary eye became a sob, and she wiped more vigorously but rallied. "And as I said before, I didn't think of it at all."

"But then at her funeral last Friday, when I was here at the church again, I saw you and remembered the envelope. The two of you were always so close. Oh, after you left the church, she would always say what a good and holy pastor you were. And I thought," sniffle, "I thought what better person to pass it on to than you?"

"Oh, dear, it's a minute to 9:00. I better get to the Fellowship Hall to start our meeting."

With what struck Danny as a most remarkable mood change, Jenny brightened and acted more like her old, cheery self as she rushed away to gather with her friends of so many years.

"There aren't more than a handful of us these days," she said over her thin shoulder as she hustled down the hall, "but we still have Henry set up for us in Fellowship Hall like it was fifty or more from the old days." And she was gone.

Danny stepped back into the lounge and looked around. He neither saw nor heard anyone else nearby. He used his dependable, old pocketknife to open the envelope. He drew out several sheets of paper, along with smaller notes and scraps, all clipped together according to size, in the neat and orderly way that Mildred always did things.

Jenny was right, he smiled to himself, *Mildred and I did work well together. Whatever compulsions for detail and order I had within me, she reinforced by always expecting me to 'have it done right, and have it done early.' Good God Almighty, I remember how she always used to say, 'It's the Lord Jesus who works miracles, Dr. Henriks, not me. If you want me to do this right for you, please get it to me earlier.' But then she would stay overtime if she had to without a complaint in order to get the job done.*

Danny sat on the Victorian love seat in the old-fashioned parlor and examined the clipped-together papers. He soon recognized that there were financial estimate sheets that were organized into large categories, and then itemized into more specific, detailed amounts. One of the sheets was entitled, "Initial Land Development Costs." The first section below the title was headed, "Purchase Price, Settlement Estimates, and Initial Permits and Fees." There were more sections with more itemizations that followed.

It didn't require a lot of head-scratching for Danny to realize that he was looking at paperwork that pertained to the acquisition of South Presbyterian Church and its acreage by what had to be Steel City Development and Design Corporation and its subsidiary, Three Rivers Contractors. The papers were obviously copies that had irregular lines across the text, as though the originals had been crumpled up and tossed away, and then later retrieved, smoothed out as well as possible, and copied.

Several smaller sheets on top of the financial documents were obviously notes scribbled in an unknown hand during more than one meeting. The notes weren't at all detailed, nor with complete sentences. More like memory-joggers. They would have been most useful to the one who authored them and would know what they were intended to remind one of. One of the note papers said simply, "All through TH, never

DL."

On top of the short stack of clipped-together sheets and notes was the smallest note of all, obviously on top to keep it from disappearing or getting lost among the larger sheets. It was written in another hand and with extremely abbreviated markings: A – 50, T – 50, T – 50, B – 100.

What could these designations mean? This one *was* a head-scratcher. *Could "A" refer to "acreage" somehow? Maybe "T" could be "timing" or "tonnage" or some other factor in the whole process? "B" could certainly be "buildings," which would be the largest development cost. The numbers could be a weighting of relative importance in developing the proposal. Or something else?*

It was crystal clear to Danny that Mildred had retrieved all these papers from somewhere, organized them over time, and had been waiting to be able to give them to someone to blow the lid off the conspiracy that was threatening the destruction of her beloved church. And the dispersal of her beloved congregation, and the unholy use of ground she considered sacred. All for the making of obscene profits and evil fortunes on the part of the devil's minions. And if one of those minions discovered what she had been doing...well, she would have to suffer a most unholy death to silence her. But they had been unable to find these papers because Mildred had given them to Jenny for safekeeping.

Danny had planned on heading down the hall to the church office and the pastor's study to drop in on Tim and have more of a conversation about the future of the church. But he decided that he needed to spend more time with these papers Mildred had left behind. He looked at his watch.

Only 9:15. Andrea, Angela and Tiny would be up by now. Maybe they've headed down for a late breakfast at the hotel, but they probably haven't left to go to the Hill yet. Maybe it will help to get three more sets of eyes looking at all this. I hope they don't mind meeting me up in Highland Park sooner.

* * *

Frank Lewis had tailed Danny from the William Penn to South Presbyterian Church. *At last, he's alone. This is the chance I've been waiting for. I'll catch him completely by surprise in the church.*

He wanted to avoid the commonly used outer door between the parking lot and the office area, so he walked casually around the building until he found a back door that was unlocked. Once inside, he would find Danny's location and set his trap.

His entry point took him into a large utility room where Henry the custodian kept his floor-polishing machine, his vacuums, mops, buckets, push brooms and dust pans, wheeled trash bins, and all kinds of other cleaning tools and supplies. Frank eased his way in, hoping not to encounter the janitor and have to make excuses for intruding upon his back room. But he saw no one and went through the door to a back hallway.

He made his way to the center of the church's offices and fellowship area, where the lounge and various meeting rooms were located. Going room by room and peering in, he encountered a small group of four people obviously meeting for some purpose. He excused himself for interrupting and moved on. He saw the five older ladies of the Dorcas Circle meeting in a little circle in the large Fellowship Hall and noted that Danny wasn't among them.

Running out of possibilities, Frank thought about searching for him in the large sanctuary area but felt quite certain that he probably wouldn't be in there. Although he hadn't wanted to, he finally went into the main office, where he spoke politely to a church member volunteer who was occupying the desk so recently vacated by Mildred. A new church secretary had not yet been hired.

"I'm an old friend of Dr. Henriks, the former pastor," Frank uttered an introduction that he considered one of the biggest lies ever to pass through his lips. "He and I had planned to meet here in the church this morning. Have you seen him?"

"Why no," the volunteer replied. "He hasn't come to the office, anyway. Do you want to wait here for him to arrive? Or shall I ask Pastor Murphy if he's seen him? Or I'll be glad to take a message if you want to leave one in case he arrives after you've gone."

"Thank you. Thank you very much, but I probably got confused about our meeting place. Oh, that's right. He and I talked about meeting here at the church, but he must have gone to the coffee shop instead. I'll head over there."

"I'm still happy to take a message, Mr...?"

"No need. Thank you." Frank left abruptly. He hurried down the hall, past the lounge, past the restrooms and a kitchenette, and out the door to the parking lot. Danny's rental car was nowhere to be seen. He was gone.

Frustration and rage started to vent upward from his volcanic core, but the cap on Devil held firm. The lava of emotion was pushed down. Frank thought calmly about his "miss."

Something caused him to leave after only fifteen minutes or so. But where has he gone now? Well, I still have the rest of today and all tomorrow to make my move and put a triumphant end to all my suffering over the better part of two decades.

He obviously loves coffee shops like Starbucks. I can scout out the nearest ones and see if he headed over to one of those. If that doesn't work, I guess I'll come back here to the church and watch to see if he returns. And if nothing else, I'll go back to the hotel and resume my vigil there. He'll go back there sometime today. Patience and discipline. Those are my constant companions.

CHAPTER EIGHTEEN

Danny had been right. His phone call to Andrea caught the three of them at breakfast at the hotel. He explained briefly what had happened, mentioning the papers that Mildred had left with Jenny and which Jenny had just given to him. Then he asked if they could meet him down his way instead of heading up to Highland Park near the seminary. Tiny and Angela both agreed, and Andrea asked where he had in mind.

"As soon as we hang up," Danny explained, "I'm going to call back to the church and ask Tim if we can drop in to talk to him after lunch today. But first I want us to meet and have the three of you get your heads together with mine and see how much sense we can make out of these papers that Mildred has identified as 'Unholy Evidence.' Then, we will hopefully have the 'smoking gun' we need to show Tim what's been going on. That there's been a high-level conspiracy all along to destroy his church. We need to bring a screeching halt to all of this before next Sunday's congregational meeting to accept the recommendation to close the church and sell off the physical assets. Why don't we meet at Smallman's Deli in Squirrel Hill? That's not far from me here, and I'll just go there and wait for you three to arrive."

Andrea promised that the three of them would get to Smallman's "ASAP." Next Danny called Tim at the church. He didn't say why he wanted to meet with Tim, but Tim didn't ask. He just said, "Sure," and that they could meet him in his study after lunch, about 1:30.

Smallman Deli on Murray Avenue in Squirrel Hill South was widely considered the premier Jewish delicatessen in the Squirrel Hill area. Its fans liked to say that it offered the best Reuben's sandwiches, corned beef and hot pastrami "west of New York City." Since the three people he loved most in his life had just had a late breakfast, Danny doubted that they would indulge in Smallman's signature offerings. But as he sat at a table for four and looked over the breakfast and brunch menu, he had to admit that both Tiny and he might have difficulty resisting the extremely delicious and hearty corned beef hash with eggs. For now, however, he ordered a pot of hot decaf coffee and settled back to look over Mildred's papers in more detail.

He was still examining, making his own notes, and trying to make sense of the "code" when Tiny, Angela and Andrea arrived at about 10:45. Tiny sat down opposite Danny and looked around as his nostrils took in the most wondrous smells. The first thing he said, even before he asked Danny what he had in front of him, was that his breakfast at the hotel had been both pricey and small for a man of his stature. Angela fixed a steely gaze at him and slammed the door shut on his prodigious appetite.

"Watch it, buster, or we're moving this session to an organic salad bar." She shook her head as Danny and Tiny went ahead and ordered a plate of the corned beef hash and eggs for each of them. "Make it a half order for the big fellow here," she instructed the server. "He already had his breakfast scarcely an hour ago."

"The same for the other one," Andrea added. When it

came to eating, Tiny and Danny were not always a good influence on each other. Angela and she had hot tea. The three listened as Danny filled them in on his brief meeting with Jenny and his examination thus far of Mildred's papers that Jenny had given him.

"Angela," he started by directing his questions to Tiny's long-time bookkeeper at Tiny's Big Security Services before he sold the business back in Traverse City. "See what you think, but it seems obvious to me that these must be rough estimates, preliminary rough drafts. I suppose showing the range of costs associated with developing the South Presbyterian Church property once Steel City Development could gain possession of the church and its land."

"Yes, I think you have to be right on that," she agreed as she perused the several pages. "What it looks like to me is what might be a first draft to be used as a starting point to meet with the key people involved in planning a future development. It's clearly not at the point of a formal estimate, yet, but could have been used to develop one. Whoever had this copy had clearly crumpled it up, probably figuring it wouldn't be needed once the more detailed, formal estimate and bid was finalized."

"Okay, good," Danny went on, "and then there are these handwritten notes which seem to me to be like somebody's personal 'shorthand.' I would call them 'memory joggers,' jotted down so that whoever wrote them could remember key points or decisions that were made in a meeting. Some of them have obviously been crumpled, too, and this one, you'll note, has a funny sort of 'fringe' on the bottom edge," he said, pointing to the note that said simply, "All through TH, never DL."

"I know what that 'fringe' is," Tiny said as he munched contentedly on a big bite of the corned beef hash. "Someone started to put the note through a shredder, but it never got past the edge of the paper. Perhaps they were in a hurry, or distracted, or just not paying attention as they were engaged in something else. But what could it mean, the notation, that is?"

"While I was waiting for you and looking at this stuff," Danny answered, "I thought about that, and it hit me like 'Duh, you dummy.' The letters are initials. 'TH' must be Todd Hickman, and 'DL' would be Dennis Lyons, the General Presbyter."

Andrea jumped on his observation. "So, the notation was something like a reminder to the person who wrote it that Dennis Lyons was to be kept out of what was going on. That everything needed to be communicated to Todd Hickman on the presbytery level."

"Precisely," Danny affirmed his own conclusion. "What we don't know, of course, is whether Dennis was being kept out of the loop to be kept in the dark. That he couldn't be allowed to know that a conspiracy was going on seeking to destroy one of the churches in his presbytery. Or whether he was fully aware and complicit but wanted to maintain that infamous 'plausible deniability.' He could be oblivious to the real dynamics of this plot. Assuming that it's really all about a struggling church that just can't keep its doors open any more. Or he could be delegating the executioner's role to his property and finance henchman, Todd Hickman.

"But the real mystery to me in these papers is this smallest note with the letters and numbers, which seems to have been written by someone else. The only thing I've been able to come up with is that it's some designation of importance, perhaps. That *acreage, title* – proper title to the land and assets, *timing* for developing the plans and making the initial steps in the development, are of roughly equal importance. But that doubly important would be the design and construction planning for the new *buildings* that would replace the old church."

Each of the other three looked at the little note. First Angela, who had been going over the figures. Then Tiny who shrugged. And finally, Andrea. After half a minute or so, Andrea announced with some hesitation, "I think I know what this is."

"What?" the other three demanded.

"I think this is a payoff note," she offered. "As was the case with 'TH' and 'DL' on the other note written by the first person, I think these designations are someone's shorthand for who's palm is to be greased with what money. An under-the-table bonus for putting this unholy scheme into action and completion. 'Alice,' the realtor, gets 50. 'Todd,' the presbytery hack, gets 50. 'Bernie' Recker, the angel investor gets 100, as a kickback, since he has the big money at stake in this development. And if I'm right about all this, there's a fourth, another 'T,' whom we haven't identified yet. Maybe a key executive at Steel City Development. But the cryptic designations remind me of simple notes that drug dealers have used in their primitive 'bookkeeping.' You know, from my old days as a State Police Sergeant on the Traverse Narcotics Team."

"And the numbers would be thousands," Tiny jumped back in enthusiastically. "Nice bonuses for an unholy trinity. And an unknown fourth."

"Well, the unknown person probably wouldn't be Alan Alderman, that CFO of Steel City, or Nate Nelson, Alice's 'ex' on the Board of Directors. Unless either one of them is such a giant force in all of this that they're nicknamed 'Tyrannosaurus,' or something," Danny added.

"You know what, though," Angela said. "When we were in the Steel City Development headquarters yesterday, I think I just happened to see that their Chief Operating Officer – wouldn't he be overseeing the different moving parts of a big project like this? – is a Thomas Thornton. He could be the other 'T.'"

"Good catch, Ang," Danny complimented her. "As the COO, he would have oversight and responsibility for all their operations, including their Development Proposal Team. He would want reports on everything, every step, every meeting. And he would personally keep control and secrecy over the whole conspiracy. He's undoubtedly getting his own little kickback for the extra diligence he has to exercise."

"Well, I don't know if we have all of this figured out," Andrea concluded, "but I think enough is clear that we can start to make a case for Pastor Tim to take to Dennis Lyons and blow the whistle on Todd Hickman. And to scuttle the project at Steel City Development and Design."

"And don't forget that *someone* apparently decided that poor Mildred knew too much and had to be silenced," Angela reminded them.

"I'd like to get these big mitts on that rat bastard," Tiny growled. "How demonic can you be, to murder an elderly church secretary because she got her hands on illicit documents? It must be someone at Steel City Development. Someone who figured that too many dollars were at stake."

Andrea frowned. "The problem is, however, that the police readily dismissed her death as an unfortunate accident. And other than Daniel's personal knowledge of Mildred and her habits, and a little indication or two like the small line of bruising on her right index finger and her box of personal things left out in the back hallway to the parking lot. Well, there doesn't seem to be any hard evidence of foul play. Let alone a viable suspect."

"I remember, dear," Danny said, "that when you were still in the Michigan State Police, you always used to talk about 'Motive.' And we certainly have that. 'Means' – she was likely lured up to the back choir loft and pushed over the low railing. 'Opportunity' – she was caught alone in the church sanctuary with no witnesses around. All we need is that 'Suspect.'"

"Oh, yah," Tiny leaned back, "just that little detail. 'Who dunnit?' Who from quite a list of nefarious characters? Unless somebody or -bodies hired a hit man for the deed."

"Wow, 'nefarious,' 'extremely wicked.' Another ten-cent word from the old street gang leader," Danny ribbed him.

"How many times have I told you in recent years that I've continued to improve myself and grow in my vocabulary?" Tiny protested in exaggerated indignation. "A man should always work to better himself. Reverend Doctor," he harrumphed.

"And you have, my friend," Danny acknowledged laughingly. "I just owe all three of you for all of that 'ruminate,' 'cows,' and 'corn' grief you gave me back at the Starbucks yesterday. But getting back to our efforts here," he turned serious again, "I think we should see if we could confront this Thomas Thornton back at Steel City. It could tell us a lot to see how he would react if he was forced to realize what we've figured out here. Maybe not the whole package, but enough to force a reaction out of him."

"Tiny, do you think that Angela and you could get in there again? I know you beat kind of a hasty retreat yesterday from that young mid-level executive in Development Proposals. But if you could get someone to call up to Thornton to let him know that you're there to discuss the church takeover with him, maybe it would force him to meet with you. If nothing else, to get a sense of how much you really know."

"We *do* have a foot in the door," Tiny smiled, "due to a grateful young security guard who helped us last time."

"It's actually more of a raised gate at the guard's booth," Angela "corrected" him. "I think he'd at least enable us to reach the front reception desk again. And we could try from there. If we tell the 'gatekeepers' that we're not leaving until we get some answers from Thornton, he would either see us to keep the noise level down or we'll end up getting familiar with more of their security personnel as we get the 'bum's rush.'"

"Okay," Danny said, "as they always say, 'nothing ventured, nothing gained.' Let's split up since we have both the Town Car and my little rental. The Joneses will head back to Steel City Development and Design to make a play on Thornton. If possible. The Henriks will drive back to the church for that 1:30 appointment with Tim Murphy. He should be one of the first to know what's being plotted against him and his congregation. That it isn't a necessary church closing that's being planned, but an orchestrated effort to line a lot of pockets with money by destroying a church. And murdering a church secretary. Let's get going."

* * *

At precisely 9:00 that Tuesday morning – as Danny had just met with Jenny Kennedy and received the envelope with Mildred's "Unholy Evidence" – Alice Nelson placed a call from her desk in the privacy of her real estate office. Thomas Thornton, COO of Steel City Development answered on his private line. A line that wasn't picked up first by an executive assistant.

"I'll make it brief," Alice spoke with lowered voice, even though no one was in her office with her.

"That would be best," the top executive replied tersely. "You should not use this number unless it's some emergency."

"I think that having those people poking at me in my own office yesterday morning may just constitute an emergency," Alice almost snapped in her anxiety and worry. "I need to know what else they're up to. And what you're prepared to do about it."

Thomas Thornton listened impatiently. *Goddamn, what a chore it is, trying to work with this bitch.*

He didn't much like real estate brokers and salespeople in the first place, and he had never liked Alice from the get-go. But she was the top elected officer in the congregation at South Presbyterian Church. Whether he liked it or not, she had a role to play as she wheeled-and-dealt for both her precious sales commission and her under-the-table bonus money. He decided on the spot to be more forthcoming with her than he really wanted to be.

"You should probably know that the Jones couple attempted to infiltrate our operation yesterday afternoon, trying to spy on us by posing as a couple who owned acreage and were looking for a development proposal from us."

"Dammit," Alice couldn't refrain from spitting into her phone. "How much did they know? What did your people tell them? What...?"

"Calm down," Thomas barked, interrupting her venting. "They were told nothing," He lied by omission. "I was informed immediately, and they exited quickly before I could have them escorted from the building and the grounds."

"Well, that's good," Alice granted. "But the one I'm really worried about is that Dr. Henriks. And his wife, she's a retired Michigan State Police sergeant, you know. South Presbyterian is his old congregation, and his nature is to keep poking until he's caused a whole lot of trouble for people like us."

This conversation has already gone on too long, Thomas thought with increasing irritation. *And there is no "people like us," bitch. You're just a real estate hack who likes her martini lunches with clients at the country club. Goddamn, my life will be better when the real estate title is transferred and recorded, and you can leave us with your pennies on the dollar and go back to smiling and swindling your pathetic clients.*

"Well, if he tries to do any more poking, either he or his friends, it's going to be a hornet's nest that he brings down on his head," Thornton growled. It wasn't his usual, sophisticated style to apply such colloquial metaphors, but it was all he could think of at her quaint use of the term, "poking."

"And you're prepared to remove them from the situation?" Alice insisted, continuing to press him.

Thomas had had enough of her aggressive, sales-oriented pushiness.

"All you and the rest of our group need to know is that I have the right person to handle the matter." He clicked off the call without bothering to say "goodbye." He transferred to a line that went to his executive assistant. "Bob," he spoke in his usual brusque manner, "if you get any future calls from an Alice Nelson, I'm not in and you don't know when I will be. Yes, but I don't care that her husband is on our board. I'll talk to him if I must, but not to her."

CHAPTER NINETEEN

Scouting out the several coffee shops in the general vicinity of the church hadn't paid off for Frank. *Well, that was a long shot, I suppose.* He grabbed a "black eye" – coffee with two shots of espresso – and a spinach and egg breakfast sandwich at the last one he checked. It would make for a light lunch and force him to stay alert as he waited. He headed back to the church.

This may be a long shot, too, but I find it hard to believe that he accomplished what he wanted to in such a short time this morning. Maybe he'll be back after his own lunch break. Otherwise, it's the hotel tonight. He parked his old blue Ford sedan in a back corner of the parking lot, hunkered down to remain unseen, and got comfortable. He replayed some of his old mental "tapes" that used to keep him from utter despair in solitary confinement. The photos of the beach in Samoa where Sarah and he were supposed to live out their lives in a tropical paradise. The gorgeous North Woods scenery of Grand Traverse Bay and towering pine trees. The chalet-like summer home where Sarah and he had spent all-too-brief a time. But that "tape" always wanted to play on to the disastrous conclusion when the two of them failed miserably in their efforts to kill Danny and dispose of his body out in the dark water of the bay.

He switched to yet another that recalled too-rare, happy days in his childhood when his sister – the one who had now cut him off – and he would play together in the yard of the mansion in Squirrel Hill. Pretending to be "superheroes" who would save humanity from alien destruction.

How ironic he thought, *that instead of saving humanity, my mission is to destroy just one person. Well, if others turn out to be "collateral damage," so be it. But when the right time presents itself, the Rev. Dr. Daniel Henriks will not be returning to Traverse City, Michigan.*

It was 12:30 when Frank settled in and started playing his mental tapes. He kept the proverbial "one eye open" in case the "long shot" paid off. A little less than an hour later, it did. Danny and Andrea drove into the church parking lot exactly five minutes before 1:30 and parked close to the side entry.

Well then, he's not alone anymore. I see he picked up the wife somewhere. But I think I need to make my move this time. I had wanted him to be alone, but didn't the two of them vow to be together "in sickness and in health...as long as we both shall live?" And how many loving couples wish, when the time comes to leave this earth, they could go together? I can grant that wish.

He looked around cautiously, didn't see anyone else either coming out of the church building just then or arriving in the parking lot. He hustled in as he had before, through the outer door into the janitor's storage room.

* * *

Danny and Andrea walked together to the church office, went in, and greeted the volunteer at the secretary's desk. She readily recognized them. Especially Danny.

"Please come in," the woman welcomed them cheerfully. "I was just going to head out for a late lunch break now that

Pastor Tim is back to answer the phone. I know that he's expecting you, so don't bother taking a seat. Just go right in, and I'll be off then."

They did as she suggested, and the woman grabbed her purse and went out of the office. Tim got up from his desk chair and greeted them warmly, shaking Danny's hand and giving Andrea a friendly hug.

"It's so good seeing you again," Tim said. "To what do I owe the pleasure of today's visit?"

Danny and Andrea had decided that it would be best if they got right to their agenda. Bring Tim up to speed on the horrible fact that the closing and selling of his church was not a result of ecclesiastical necessity and responsible stewardship. But rather a real estate and development scheme driven by immense greed and subterfuge. That the very people with whom he had been working so closely, Alice, Todd, Bernie, Alan and now Thomas Thornton, had all been conspiring together and using him and the church for their own financial ends.

"And look at these papers that poor Mildred had retrieved and copied," Danny handed them to Tim after opening the white envelope he was carrying. Tim noted the cursive writing in Mildred's hand on the front of the envelope.

"I see she labeled it 'Unholy Evidence,'" Tim remarked as he began to look over the papers. "And I see what she meant. It's apparent that well before we started meeting together to discuss the future of the church, that future had already been determined by these development interests. In collusion with both Alice and the presbytery as represented by Todd Hickman."

"But not with Dennis Lyons' involvement, it appears from that one note," Andrea pointed out. "Or if he was involved, he wanted to distance himself from the 'dirty work.'"

"I'm horrified that people professing to have the church's

best interest at heart would be so unchristian and callous about the faithful members of this congregation, their ministries and missions." Tim shook his head with obvious distress. "We're all supposed to be servants of Jesus Christ."

"Well, I'm afraid that some of these people care only about serving money. Remember, what the old King James Version used to call 'mammon,' evil money?" Danny concluded.

"Yes, yes," Tim said, "the Sermon on the Mount, Matthew 6:24, 'You cannot serve both God and mammon.' Well, thank you for bringing this to me. What do you make of this small note with the individual letters and numbers attached to them?"

Andrea spoke to that. "I'm pretty sure that the letters refer to the first initials of those key players in this conspiracy, and that the numbers represent under-the-table payoff sums in the thousands: fifty thousand 'bonus' dollars to Alice Nelson, fifty to Todd Hickman, one hundred to key investor Bernie Recker, and we think the remaining fifty to Thomas Thornton, the Chief Operating Officer of Steel City Development and Design. The note obviously was made by Alan Alderman, the Chief Financial Officer with whom you are acquainted. He would have had responsibility for finding ways to make the 'bonuses' and keep them off the books of the corporation."

"And all of this has come to light because our old church secretary, Mildred, suspected that all was not right, and she managed to retrieve these papers out of trash after secret meetings here at the church," Tim confirmed.

"So it would appear," Danny agreed. "Part of the mystery is how the person's notes, and Alan's payoff code, ended up in trash with the rough drafts of the financial figures. But somehow Mildred got them."

"And I'm very grateful that now I have them," Tim said.

"You can rest assured that..." His statement was interrupted by a tall, gaunt man who stepped into the Pastor's Study, slammed and locked the door behind him, and swung a Beretta M9 9mm pistol back and forth at the three of them. Not wanting to be recognized at first, Frank wore a white, devilish mask that made him seem more ominous.

"Nobody get up. Not a word, not a flinch, or I empty the magazine into all of you. I have three rounds for each of you. Very slowly reach into your pockets – and you, Mrs. Henriks, into your purse. Slowly toss your cell phones over at my feet. I'm not kidding. I will shoot to kill if anyone tries anything."

Andrea, Tim and Danny were all totally taken by surprise and shocked by this invasion. The identity of this stranger was yet another mystery...except that the height, the general complexion, the hair color, and especially the voice, awoke some glimmer of recognition in Danny's memory. It had been quite a few years, but he finally asked.

"Frank? Frank Lewis...is it you behind that mask?"

CHAPTER TWENTY

Frank had seen the volunteer secretary go out to her car and drive off for her lunch break. There were no meetings going on that Tuesday afternoon, and the custodian worked only part-time now due to budget cuts. So, he had gone home at noon. The only remaining cars were those of Pastor Tim Murphy, the rental car driven by Danny Henriks, and Frank's car in the back corner, where church members and others might leave a car for a time while they went off in someone else's car.

The first thing that Frank had done was go around and use the hanging Allen wrench to crank up all the "panic bars" on the outer doors around the church. That would keep anyone arriving at the church from entering and complicating his mission. Unless it was one of the few members to have a key. He then did a quick walk-around to check the various rooms and even the big sanctuary, just to make sure that there wasn't someone, or more than one someone, doing something in the church after having walked there or been dropped off. All was empty.

Satisfied that the only people besides himself to be in the church just then were the pastor, Danny and Andrea, Frank had snuck into the church office, locked that outer door with its deadbolt, and crept to listen at the door of the Pastor's

Study. Within a few minutes he was able to confirm that he heard all three voices in the study. He donned the mask, slipped the Beretta out of his waistband, gripped the door handle, opened it fast, and stepped in with the pistol leveled at the three around the desk.

He had them. He had *him*.

* * *

"Yes, Rev. Dr. Daniel Henriks, it's Frank Lewis. Back from hell but bringing it with me for your personal enjoyment." He removed the mask.

Tim started to rise from behind his desk, but Frank angrily ordered him back in his seat.

"I said nobody gets up. Not a twitch. Or I fire. You, too, Mrs. Henriks. Stay put."

"Did you get paroled, Frank," Danny asked, "or did you actually escape from Ionia?"

"Parole, Danny Boy. I became a model prisoner. The poster boy for rehabilitation. Deemed no longer a threat to society. You would have believed in me yourself. I went to chapel. To visiting clergy prayer services. To Bible study. To support groups for recovering addicts. Anything, and everything, to earn that parole. All so that I could get out. And. Hunt. You. Down."

"How did you know to find me here in Pittsburgh instead of in Northern Michigan?"

"I didn't, actually," Frank didn't mind admitting. "I came here to collect an old debt before going back to Michigan to find you. But then your old church secretary met her violent end that Friday. I just knew that you would have to come here for her funeral. So, you were delivered right to me, you see. Karma is sweet, isn't it?"

"Well, if it's me you want," Danny offered, "let Andrea and

Pastor Tim go. They've done nothing to you."

"No," Andrea shouted. "I'm not leaving you, Daniel."

"How touching," Frank sneered. "But actually, Danny, I'll give you half of your bargain. Pastor, I have no beef with you. Slowly, no sudden moves now, get up from your chair and ease over to your personal powder room over there. As I warned you before, if you so much as twitch in my direction, I'll put your three slugs into you before you can complete the first step."

Tim did as he was instructed and moved very slowly and carefully toward the small restroom. He paused at the door and looked at Frank.

"Go on. Get in there. And close the door behind you," Frank ordered.

Once Tim was inside, Frank quickly noted that the door hinges were on the outside, facing the larger office.

Good, he won't be able to pop the pins to get out of there. Still holding onto the Beretta, Frank walked over to the small conference table, grabbed a chair, and carried it over to the restroom door. Glancing ominously over at where Danny and Andrea were still seated in front of the desk, he then turned and jammed the top of the back of the chair under the doorknob of the restroom. He jiggled and shoved the chair to make sure that it was jammed securely and wouldn't come loose and fall over if Tim tried to force his way out of the restroom.

While Frank was occupied for a few seconds, Danny calculated their limited options.

He's too far away for me to rush him. As soon as I was out of my chair he would turn and fire. We would never get out of here in time before he could shoot. Our only recourse is to get him off-balance and buy a couple of seconds. Danny looked quickly at the desktop and chose his item. *I only get one shot at this. So don't "try," Danny Boy. "Do."*

He looked intently at Andrea and silently mouthed the words, "Get ready to run."

Just as Frank gave his last jiggle to the jammed chair, Danny reached over the desktop, grabbed a heavy, solid glass paperweight, and in virtually the same motion fired it at Frank's head. His old pitching aim was on target. The paperweight struck Frank hard in his forehead, stunning him for an instant. It caused him to drop the handgun he had been holding awkwardly while gripping the chair back.

For the briefest split-second Danny's brain thought about lunging for the Beretta, but it had fallen straight down at Frank's feet. And although he was reeling a bit unsteadily, he quickly bent over and picked it up. So instead, Danny stuck to his original plan. He grabbed Andrea's hand. The two of them dashed for the office door. He threw back the deadbolt and flung the door open. They rushed into the main office. Danny had the presence of mind to grab the door as they went through it and slam it back shut before Frank could take aim and fire.

The two of them kept going and ran out of the Church Office and into the hallway, in the direction of the parking lot. Down at the end of the hall, however, he was alarmed to see two older ladies standing just outside the glass door. They were peering in and appearing curious as to why they couldn't get into the church.

If we keep going in that direction, he assessed the situation, *and Frank steps out into the hall and shoots, one of those innocent women could be hit...if he misses us.*

"Come on," he ordered Andrea. "We have to run into the sanctuary."

They got to the hallway corner where Mildred had set down her box of personal things before she headed toward the sanctuary to investigate the strange buzzing noise. Danny and Andrea dashed down the hallway to the sanctuary and opened the door. They headed into the large worship center with its rows of pews, tall stained-glass windows, and very high, arched ceiling.

"Duck down," Andrea had the presence of mind to give her own order, "we can't let him see which way we've gone. But where *are* we going, now that we're in here?"

Once again Danny had mentally listed their options for a getaway.

The only doors out of the sanctuary besides the one we just used are the main doors to the front walk, which have panic bars but are also key-locked so that they can't be opened from either side without a key. And the outer door off the chancel which is primarily a fire escape door. But it too has both a panic bar and a lock that prevents it from being opened from either side.

"We only have one choice," he whispered as they crouched and scurried in between pews. "There's an old, abandoned Pastor's Study at the end of the back choir loft. It's left over from the original architect's design for the church. From back in the days when pastors often liked to have a 'retreat' where they could withdraw from the daily, mundane business of the church. Go up to privacy and quiet, pray and work on their sermons, be close to God and the angels up high in the sanctuary...."

"Daniel!" Andrea whispered almost in a panic.

She's right. If there was ever a time that didn't allow for one of my "lectures," this would be it.

He shut up for once and led her up the same steps that Mildred had used to find the irritating buzz in the high choir loft. In the meantime, they had heard Frank come through the door they had used to enter the sanctuary. He had wasted a minute or so checking the hallways outside the Church Office to make sure that they had not run into some other part of the church building. But he finally and rightly concluded that they must have gone into the sanctuary.

"Danny Boy...Andrea...." Frank coaxed. "Come out, come out, wherever you are." He waited and listened for just a few seconds. All was quiet. "Tell you what, Danny, I'll forgive the bump you put on my forehead. You were desperate and would try anything. And I'll overlook your pathetic attempt to escape me. Present yourself to me for your 'just desserts,' and I won't bother finding your precious Andrea to deliver her present of three taps to the back of her graying head."

"You don't have any choice, you know. I've checked. You can't exit through any door except the one we just used. And that requires a pass from me. I'll give that pass to Mrs. Henriks. I already have my 'get out of jail free' card," he chortled. "Just have the guts to take your punishment like a rotten sinner should. Devil demands what's due."

Frank stopped and listened intently once more. *They're in here somewhere. They have to be.* Finally, he was rewarded with the faint squeak of rusty hinges from somewhere up in the choir loft. *Gotcha,* he grinned evilly. He climbed the steps to the choir loft. *They've really cornered themselves now. At last, this will be over, and I will have prevailed.*

CHAPTER TWENTY-ONE

The old pastor's study, up high at the end of the choir loft, hadn't been used as a study for many years. The last time had been a number of pastorates ago. More modern times had taken the studious, prayerful, almost-cloistered pastor out of his "on high" retreat and down into the "action" of the church business. He or she had to be accessible, available at a moment's notice to the urgent needs and little whims of his or her members, "in the middle" of whatever was going on in the church. Consequently, the old study had become nothing more than a storage space. It was full of discarded old furniture, boxes, many items that should have been trashed long ago, and an abundance of cobwebs and accumulated dust.

Temporarily, until Frank reached it, it was Andrea and Danny's "panic room." However, there was no way to keep Devil out. There was not even a lock on the old, wooden door. The old skeleton key had been lost long ago, and there wasn't anything in there that needed protection and security anyhow.

Until the Henriks showed up.

Danny looked around for something to use as a defensive weapon for when Frank would burst through the door. All he saw was an old, broken broom. *At least the handle could be a club or a spear,* he thought as optimistically as he could. He grabbed it and got ready to strike, while Andrea looked around for something more formidable.

"Have you found anything?" Danny whispered anxiously.

"Not much," Andrea had to admit. "Just this old pulpit Bible. Weighs a ton. No wonder the old pastors had somebody carry it down the center aisle for them."

Danny's brain was so habitual that he instantly thought of the more modern term for such a person – quite descriptively, "Bible Bearer" – but refrained from saying it and stayed focused on their plight.

"Well, I wish you still went into dicey situations with your snub-nosed revolver in your ankle holster," he said regretfully. "We could use it about now."

Frank wasn't about to rush recklessly through the closed door, however. *Danny Boy's surely going to try to jump me if I burst in there. Who knows what he's found in there to try to fight me with. Devil's not that stupid.*

With an announcement that totally surprised Danny and Andrea, Frank shouted through the closed door, "Stand back and to the side. I'm firing through the door."

He didn't want to cheat himself by having Danny especially struck by a wild bullet. So, after a few seconds to allow them to clear away, he let go with three rounds through the wooden door. One about head-high, one chest-high, and one waist high. Or perhaps head-high if either of them had been crouching down. Then, before either of them had a chance to jump back toward the door, he gave it a powerful kick, stopped it from swinging back on himself, and stepped into the old study. Once again swinging his gun, ready to shoot in a flash.

"Drop it or I shoot her," Devil commanded Danny as he clutched the broom handle and held it up to take a swing.

Danny had no reasonable choice. Frank had the gun trained on Andrea, standing to one side, still clutching the old, over-sized, leather-bound pulpit Bible with both hands and straining to keep a hold on it. Danny let the broom handle clatter to the floor.

"I have to admit," Devil sneered with dark humor, "this is indeed an appropriate time to seek solace and comfort from Holy Scripture, but you can set that down on the floor, sweetie. A Bible study is not on the schedule of the day. This is a time for action, not idle reflection."

The heavy book thudded as she let it fall to the floor.

"Now, we seem to be back where we started in Pastor Tim's study. Only, this time, I don't need to deal with him. So, his three rounds could be used to clear my path into this room where you've run out of options. Entirely. Not a move," he barked as Danny reflexively flinched as though he was going to try to charge Frank. "You'll get your chance in just a moment here, but first..." He looked around the old study, past the discarded furniture and stacked up boxes, and fixed his stare on a side closet where the old-time pastors used to hang their pulpit robes, stoles, and other vestments. The door was closed. But this time the old skeleton key was conveniently sticking out of the keyhole.

"Andrea, step around the Word of God discarded on the floor there and go unlock that closet door. Now open the door, step in, and close it behind you. I don't need you to be here right now. And Danny Boy, as soon as she's in there and has closed the door behind her, you will go over there and turn the key, locking her away in safety." Devil had learned that he didn't need to do it himself and create another moment of vulnerability.

Although he was worried to the extreme about what Frank had in mind, at least Danny wasn't quite so troubled about complying with this order. If Frank's intention was to take Andrea out of the action and harm's way, *that*, at least, was something he could agree with.

"Don't do this, Daniel," Andrea pleaded through the shut door as he turned the key. Even if confinement in the closet offered her safety from whatever Frank had in mind, she didn't want to be separated from Danny. And she feared more than words could express what might happen to him.

"Patience...patience and faith," he whispered with his mouth close to the door.

"Again, how touching," Devil mocked. "Now, finally, it's just you and me, Rev. Doctor, so can we talk? You don't have to answer that. What you want most of all in this critical moment is to keep me talking. And, not shooting. You've always been good with math, so you know that I have three bullets for each of you remaining in this magazine and chamber. Or I suppose six for you, and we keep the Mrs. 'closeted.'"

On the devil's black heart, I love these metaphors, he congratulated his own wittiness.

"Okay, Frank, let's talk," Danny said grimly. "In fact, why don't we start with why you're doing this. Is it so obsessively stupid, as being fixated on completing my murder? The one you failed so miserably at, when Sarah Brand was your mistress. You were her lap dog, of course. Or is it just that you've been plotting and dreaming of your revenge all those years in prison because you were foiled in trying to murder me? Or are you back in your pathetic quest at the service of the big money interests who are determined to destroy this church and replace it with luxury condos and townhouses, the likes of which they would never admit you into?"

Devil knew full well that Danny was deliberately trying to get under his tough skin. To pry the cap off his caldera of explosive lava. To get him to "lose his cool" and react rashly. To make a bad mistake. But he wouldn't be so stupid as to fall for it.

"Big money interests out to destroy the church and

replace it with development? You know, Danny Boy, I got the idea in the last few days that something like that must be afoot. But no, I have nothing to do with that. My mission is far too important, far too 'righteous,' to use your language, to lower myself to the status of a hired gun."

In the devil's name, I love those metaphors.

"But I'll answer your question. After all, a man who's about to meet his Maker and be condemned for all eternity should pass through the door of death with a fatal appreciation of why he's being sent through it. In the proverbial nutshell, I experienced hell on earth my entire life. From early childhood abuse and neglect to the complete destruction of my love and my dreams, and I prevailed. I survived. I was stronger in the isolation of my life than what was heaped upon me by an evil God and his angels of misery. Until you came along. You deliberately turned Sarah's head. You got in between her love and mine. You sided with her abusive husband and insisted upon solving the murder of the Rev. Dr. Bill Brand instead of letting his deserved death rest as a simple suicide. You ruined everything! And karma has delivered you into my hand at last."

Danny kept quiet during Frank's tirade. Frank had been right about one thing. So long as he was talking, he wasn't shooting...yet. He seriously doubted that he could reason with such a volcanic pool of molten, white-hot hate, but he had to try.

"Frank..." He started.

"Don't call me Frank right now," Devil cut him off, "for the sake of imposing judgment on you, I'll go by how I got dubbed in that hellhole of a prison, 'the devil's own.' Devil for short. He's my deity now, and it's his work I'm about to do."

Danny wasn't about to honor that order. "I wasn't trying to steal Sarah from you, Frank. I didn't want her. Our relationship was long ago. Way back in our undergraduate days. We went our separate ways. She chose Bill Brand over me. Sure, something of our friendship still existed, but not any measure of love or desire. On my part, certainly."

"Don't lie to me," Devil gripped the gun handle harder so that his knuckles showed white. "I learned far too late that it was actually you that she wanted to go off to the South Seas with on Brand's money."

"I can't speak to that," Danny insisted, "only that it was not my wish or plan. I only wanted to figure out who killed Bill. And why."

Devil remained unconvinced. He had lived too long in too much pain and suffering to allow any other interpretation of the events that had happened than the one that fueled his explosive rage. The discussion had wearied his mind, and he wasn't about to let his terrible resolve weaken or alter. It was time to put a triumphant end to his righteous quest.

With no warning or indication of what he intended to do, Devil swung the gun in the direction of the closet door and fired a round through the center panel of the door, resulting in a terrified scream from Andrea inside.

"Andrea, honey, are you hurt? Did he hit you?" Danny called out in a panic.

"No. I'm okay. It was close. Right by my ear. But it missed," she answered.

Devil swung the gun right back on Danny as soon as he had squeezed off the shot.

"Now here's what's going to happen," he said with utter coldness. "There are five more rounds in this gun. And while two of them have Andrea's name on them, and three have yours, I'm going to be more merciful than that evil God in heaven. I'm going to set my gun on this box right behind me, and you can come and get it. Or die trying."

"I'm not going to fight you, Frank," Danny rejected his

deal. "It makes no sense. I never intended any harm for you. I never did anything to cause your pain and suffering. And I don't intend to do it now."

Devil swung the gun back in the direction of the closet door and quickly fired off a second shot. Then he pointed it back at Danny.

"Oh, God," Danny wailed, "Andrea...."

"I'm still okay," she called out with a quaver in her frightened voice. After the first shot through the door, she had crouched down as low as she could and tried to huddle behind a box on the closet floor.

"Now there are four bullets left," Devil declared. "And I've just reassigned one of yours to her. Two rounds for each of you, and I'm not taking any more wild shots. The next two will be in her head, and then two in yours. Unless you want to take your chances and come get this gun." He reached back and put the gun on top of the box, just inside the old study door. "You can come and get it, use all four bullets on me, and the two of you walk sweetly out that door behind me. What a deal," he smiled devilishly.

Danny didn't want to take his deal or have anything to do with the twisted mind and blackened heart of this soulless man, but he had run out of choices and options. He tensed for a second and then lunged in Frank's direction, hard at his chest.

It was what Devil had wanted all along, what kept him alive and hopeful all those years. He was ready. He met Danny's desperate charge with hardened muscles and honed reflexes. He twisted his cat-like body to one side, deflected the wild swing Danny took at his head, pushed Danny off-balance as he brushed Devil's chest with his shoulder, and then got behind Danny and placed his sinewy left forearm across Danny's throat. It was much the same move that he had made on the street thug back in Detroit that evening. But he didn't get the neck-snapping grip with his powerful right hand. Not yet.

Devil pinned Danny's body with his free right arm, while maintaining constricting pressure on Danny's windpipe with his left. Danny flailed both of his arms and tried to claw at Frank's choking left arm with his own left hand. He failed to make any headway at freeing himself. He then tried stomping on Frank's foot or shin with his right heel. Devil was taller, however, and he leaned back powerfully and kept Danny off-balance, at times on his tiptoes, straining to find traction and always struggling to breathe.

Devil's application of force to the throat and windpipe was calculated and disciplined. He applied just enough pressure to constrict the airway, and to slow blood to the brain, but not enough to kill. Or for that matter, to keep Danny from being able to whisper huskily an occasional word.

Danny could feel his strength ebbing and his brain getting woozy.

Devil felt great. This long-anticipated moment was like a once-in-a-lifetime religious experience. It was better than he could have imagined. He felt ecstasy. He felt exhilarated. He even thought to himself in the context of his old Christian life and faith: *Is this how Saul of Tarsus – Paul the Apostle – felt when the Spirit knocked him from horseback on the Road to Damascus? Overwhelmed with divine power? Was it anything like this for John Wesley, when he came down from his experience of revelation and said that he was "strangely warmed?" This is life-giving power and spiritual warmth for me...and life-ending power and the fire of hell for Daniel Henriks? O Devil, how wonderful this religious experience.*

He couldn't resist whispering cruelly into the ear of the fading Danny, "And do you have any last words? Say it. Confess the cause of my agony and suffering." He started to squeeze the last, irresistible leverage on Danny's throat. He listened for those precious "last words" to be whispered before any ability to make sound was lost forever to Danny.

The words came. In a whisper barely audible Danny confessed the name of the person who had been the focal point of Frank's abject misery. "Sarah B-Brand."

For only the second time in Frank's tortured life an epiphany occurred. It was totally unexpected and caught him absolutely unprepared to receive it. Far more powerful than the epiphany that changed his prison experience, this expression of Truth was like a beam of indescribable divine light and power that shot into the cosmos from far beyond, from the center of heaven itself. *This* was true religious experience like the one that transformed St. Paul or John Wesley. This was spiritual power and searing, white-hot heat. This was Conversion. It was as though the Angel Gabriel wrote on the white board of his mind and soul.

It was Sarah Brand who destroyed your life...and you let her...but still God loves you and forgives you.

Like the sight that was restored to the blind man on the roadside outside Jericho, or the scales that fell from the eyes of Saul of Tarsus so that he could become Paul the Apostle, Frank clearly *saw* the truth about his life. And that he was unjustly choking the life out of an innocent man. He immediately relaxed his relentless leverage and Danny collapsed onto the floor, barely able to gasp for air. Frank stood above him as he slumped on the floor, but the former devil's own, if anything, felt even more weak and helpless than Danny did. He couldn't seem to move or speak in the absolute stripping-away of his consuming hate and lust for vengeance.

Frank didn't even seem to notice that Andrea had managed to jostle the bullet-ridden closet door open and now rushed to hold Danny. When he had appeared to comply with Frank's order and locked her in the closet, Danny had turned the key only part-way, the lock only partly catching, in hopes that the opportunity would arrive for her to free herself. Frank was incapable of thinking about any of that. He felt totally, spiritually naked before God, totally unworthy of mercy and forgiveness. But somehow forgiven and redeemed with new faith and life. It was far too soon for him to be able to voice the words of repentance to Danny and Andrea. He could only stare in utter sorrow for his sin and reach a trembling hand down to help Danny to his feet. For the first time in his life, Frank experienced genuine love for others.

Frank touched Danny and reached under his armpit to lift him. Andrea was so shocked and somehow grateful that she failed to recoil from his gesture. Then a shot was fired from behind them.

CHAPTER TWENTY-TWO

Frank Lewis fell dead on the old study floor. The Angel of Death swept up his freshened soul as blood and life trickled out of him. The shooter had slipped through the unlocked door and silently grabbed the Beretta off the box where Frank put it before his fight with Danny.

Andrea bent over Danny as he struggled to regain consciousness. She tried to encourage and help him to get up. Neither of them saw the shooter until the shot was fired and Frank's lifeless body fell practically on top of Danny.

Danny couldn't quite get the words to form from his damaged larynx, but Andrea blurted out, "Tim...Tim, how did you...you shot Frank?"

"Yes, Frank, that old assistant rector to Bill Brand at the Episcopal Church of the Resurrection," Tim said with a casualness that was completely out-of-place for the situation of the pastor of South Presbyterian Church killing a man in the church building.

Danny tried to clear his throat and get a few words out as he struggled to his feet.

"Here, Tim, the gun...hon, call police." He reached out to take the Beretta M9 from Tim's hand, who was still holding it as though in shock at his deed.

"Oh, no. I don't think so for any of that." Tim stepped back and spoke in no uncertain manner. "I'll keep the gun thank you. And there won't be any call to the police. At least not until I'm ready to make it."

"Tim, it's over." Danny cleared his throat and managed to speak hoarsely. "You shot him dead. We're all safe now."

The new situation started to dawn on Andrea. "I don't think Tim stepped in to save us, Daniel. What's going on, Tim?"

"Okay," Tim drew a breath. "Why don't you two sit down again and I'll tell you. Why not? There's no rush here. No one is getting into the church. A deranged murderer locked everyone out so that he could kill the three of us in his psychotic rage. They were going to be random, senseless murders. But after he shot the two of you up here, I managed to wrest the gun away and shot him dead, thus escaping his violent intent."

"Tim, I...I...don't understand." Danny was still trying to clear his head and regain his voice.

"Your old associate pastor, colleague and friend intends to kill us, himself," Andrea concluded for him.

"But why?" Danny couldn't make sense of what he was hearing. "We were here to help you and your church. And if you weren't saving us from Frank Lewis, why did you shoot him instead of letting him kill us for you?"

"I was totally surprised that Frank Lewis showed up here today," Tim said. "For me he is proving to be a godsend. It was up to me to find a way to get rid of you. And he came along to become the perfect patsy. This is his gun. He will prove to be the one who murdered you. And I will get away with yet another murder."

"Another murder?" Danny couldn't believe what he was hearing. His foggy mind was still having difficulty processing it all.

"It was you," Andrea said. "You killed Mildred. Why kill your loyal church secretary?"

"Yes. I pushed Mildred over the railing down to the pews below. The meddling old bag. Okay, let's start from the beginning. Not that I owe you an explanation, but this is rather fun. I didn't come here to revitalize this stupid church. I hate this church."

"Why?" Danny was stunned at every word that was coming from Tim's mouth.

"Because it was here that I lost the love of my life. On our wedding day. If you hadn't become the target of people who wanted to kill you, Danny, that sniper would never have shot Mark to death. It should have been you on the receiving end of that bullet when death crashed our wedding. Being your go-fer and flunky ended up costing me my life's partner. I hate this church. And you along with it."

"So then why did you agree to be called back to become the pastor?" Andrea asked.

"Simple," Tim said. "I knew that real estate people and developers were desperate to obtain property in this South Pittsburgh area in order to build. In fact, as you know, I've always been an avid golfer. One day over drinks at the 19th hole of the South Pittsburgh Country Club, I teased Thomas Thornton, of Steel City Development and Design, about how much would it be worth to him if he was able to get his hands on prime acreage in this area.

"He thought for a moment and then asked me how such a thing might be possible. I suggested that it could be possible if a certain Presbyterian church happened to close its doors and be sold by the presbytery. He told me to let him know if that could truly happen."

"But how did you get Pittsburgh Presbytery to play ball with such a devious idea?" Andrea wondered.

"At the time I was doing interim pastor work at smaller

churches in the Greater Pittsburgh area, and since more than one of them had shaky finances and uncertain futures, I ended up spending a lot of time with a certain chairman of the presbytery's Property and Finance Committee..."

"Todd Hickman." Danny had no trouble figuring out that detail, despite his fogginess.

"Bingo," Tim confirmed. "And after different late meetings at these small churches over a few years, Todd and I would relax with a drink or two at a local bar before going home. One time he was feeling down about personal matters, and being lubricated by a few scotch and waters, he let his guard down and confessed that his wife and he were financially strapped. He desperately needed a cash infusion.

"I suggested to Todd that if he would care to pull some strings with Dennis Lyons and the Committee on Ministry and get me called to be the pastor of South Presbyterian, he could get that money he so desperately needed. I warned him that it would take a while. But he said that his debt load wasn't going away any time soon, so the money would be welcome whenever it came."

"All right." Danny was following Tim's narrative better now. "So, you recruited Todd to join the Destroy South Presbyterian team. But wouldn't Dennis have caught wind of this scheme?" he said huskily.

"That part was rather easy. Todd and I met with Dennis one day and suggested that since South Presbyterian was one of the several struggling churches in the presbytery, if the leadership of the presbytery and the congregation would partner and arrange for me to become the new pastor, I would both develop new and exciting ministries and mission to the South Pittsburgh area *and* help the present congregation to make the transition into closing the church and selling off the unneeded physical assets. It didn't hurt that many thousands of dollars would go to the presbytery and help lift other churches in need."

"But you needed a key person or two in the congregation itself to play ball with you," Andrea added.

"Exactly right," Tim confirmed. "Thornton and his buddy at Steel City Development, Alan Alderman, the CFO, knew that one of their directors, Nate Nelson, had a wife in real estate. Alice, as you know, was a long-time member of this church, but she would sell off her widowed mother's house and put mom in a nursing home for a big commission. So, Thomas and Alan approached Alice over cocktails at the club one day. She was a more than willing recruit. It really sealed the deal for us when we sat down with church member Bernie Recker and convinced him that we had his next great investment opportunity. He agreed wholeheartedly. I know this sounds like a whole lot of skullduggery, but...."

Despite their perilous plight, Danny couldn't help himself, he made a low side comment to Andrea, "See, I'm not the only one...."

Tim looked curious but went on enjoying his narrative.

"With Todd, Thomas and Alan, Alice and Bernie – and me, of course – we had the necessary players to move to dissolution of the congregation, closing of the church, and having the presbytery sell off the buildings and grounds to Steel City Development."

"But Mildred somehow caught on to what you were all up to." Andrea said.

"In retrospect, I suppose it risked opening us up to a meddling busybody like Mildred to have a couple of our meetings here at the church. But Alan and Alice wanted to see the buildings and grounds first-hand from a sales deal approach. And Bernie wanted so much to show them around."

"But wouldn't Alice already know the church well from her years of membership and involvement on the Session as an elder?" Andrea continued.

"Sure," Tim agreed, "but she had never looked at it from a 'sell it off and collect the money' standpoint. As greedy as Alice is, she wanted to make sure that she got every dollar she could off a commission on an agreed-upon sales price between the presbytery and Steel City Development."

The words "every dollar" resonated in Danny's clearing head.

"Dollars," he said. "That under-the-table payoff bonus note Mildred found: 'A' was for Alice, 'T' for Todd, 'B' for Bernie...but the other 'T' was you! We thought it stood for Thomas Thornton."

"Well, that's where your vaunted investigative skills failed you," Tim sneered. "Yes, it stood for me. Think about it. Why would a 'bonus' go to either Alan or Thomas? It was their money, Steel City Development money, that was paying off the coalition members. The corporation would take care of them separately, in the form of their usual annual bonuses for 'good performance.' The fifty thousand for the second 'T' was to be mine."

"And you would sell out your own congregation and murder poor Mildred for a measly fifty thousand dollars?" Andrea spit out her contempt.

"Hell yes," Tim said. "I would do it for five dollars. This church – and you, Danny, you – ruined my life by taking away the one person I loved more than any other. And Mildred shouldn't have been sticking her nose in where it didn't belong. Oh, I admit that part of the problem was of my own making. I got sloppy. After the second of our group's meetings here at the church, I took the rough draft proposal papers and my personal short-hand notes back to my desk down in the Pastor's Study and crumpled them up and put them in the wastebasket.

"After a short while, I got called away by a young church

member who had come by the church to look in the sanctuary to visualize her wedding day. And while I was talking to her down there, it dawned on me that it was careless simply to put those papers and notes in the trash for Henry to collect. Not that he would have noticed or thought about anything, probably. I went back and smoothed them out and put them through the office shredder. But in the meantime, meddling Mildred must have slipped into my study, pulled them out of the wastebasket and made copies, returning the crumpled originals to the wastebasket before I came back in."

"So, what alerted you to her interference in your perfect plan?" Danny had to know.

"It was Alan's little payoff bonus notation." Tim didn't mind disclosing that detail. "When I crumpled up the papers and tossed them in the wastebasket, I noticed his little note. I must have scooped it up inadvertently after our meeting and gathered it in with my papers. We had been sitting next to each other, you see. Well, when I hastened back into my study to shred those possibly incriminating papers, I couldn't find Alan's note among them. I knew absolutely for certain that it had been there. so it dawned on me that Mildred must have smoothed out the papers, copied them, re-crumpled them, replaced them in my wastebasket...but forgot to include Alan's code."

"So, you figured that she was on to your skullduggery," Danny went on, "and that you couldn't risk having her take it any further. So, your demonic little coalition decided that she had to be eliminated. And how did you accomplish that? I know full well that Mildred suffered from acrophobia and would not have wanted to go up into the choir loft out there without a strong compulsion to do so."

"I was well aware of that, also." Tim acted rather huffy that Danny seemed to imply something he might not know.

"But you may or may not know that in her natural fussiness she also hated things like nagging, incessant, repetitive noises. Just before she left the office on her final Friday, I snuck up here to the choir loft and tied a burner cell phone with an alarm function to the kids' banner. I tucked it under the edge of the banner so that it couldn't be seen from down below in the pews and set off the timer on 'loud.' Damn thing was almost like a fire alarm." Tim chortled at his own cleverness.

"I knew," he continued, "that she was too compulsive just to leave and let the thing buzz away like that. Besides, she would be terribly curious as to what the hell was going on. So, I actually hid in here – in the old, long-abandoned pastor's study – and waited until she had to climb the steps, go over to the railing, and try to untie the irritating cell phone to turn it off. It worked like a charm." Tim actually congratulated himself on his devilish success. "As she screwed up her courage and suppressed her phobia and reached over to untie it, I silently snuck up behind her, gave her the old heave-ho, and over she went."

"It surprised me, I must admit, that as she went over the railing, her finger caught in the string I had used to tie the cell phone, gave her just the slightest jerk against the outer wall of the loft, and she looked back up as it snapped, and she fell to her certain death. I believe she had the briefest flash of recognition that it was I who had pushed her over. Oh well, maybe it gave her a last, split-second satisfaction to at least know who it was that put an end to her nosy meddling. I don't think she ever really liked me, anyway, Danny. She had such a thing for you as her old boss. Never gave me much of a chance, nor much respect."

"Anyway, I untied the loose end of the string from the banner, went down and checked. She was a goner. I picked up the broken cell phone with the other end of the string attached. I made sure, of course, that no one else was around to see me leave and drive away from the church. There was absolutely no evidence that I had been there at that time, let alone had anything to do with her death. It was all so pure and perfect that it felt downright holy."

Both Danny and Andrea found it nauseating to sit and listen to Tim's callous and hateful words. Danny couldn't help but shake his head sadly.

Andrea spoke up. "You clearly don't have the first clue as to what the word 'holy' means, Tim Murphy. I have never heard anything so evil and demonic in my life. You're never going to get away with this."

"And you're sure as hell never going to collect those fifty thousand dollars," Danny interrupted. "Let alone be able to spend it to feed your rotten soul. You're going to rot in hell for your crimes and your sin."

Andrea's verbal attack and Danny's assault knocked Tim's composure off-center. Infuriated at their defiance, he shot a round into the floor at their feet, and then swung the Beretta at each of them, commanding their stillness.

"Well, now we get to the part where you go to hell first, both of you. I've come to understand so well, Danny Boy, why you've had a whole club of people wanting to kill you over the years. How in the name of all that's unholy you avoided your own demise is beyond me, but accomplishing it is certainly not beyond my ability. You end. Today. Now."

"The last club member gunning for you before me – this Frank Lewis on the floor here – has given me the perfect cover story. He locked me in the downstairs pastor's restroom. Too bad for him he didn't know that there was a spare key stored inside. And then he chased the two of you up here, shot through the door to the choir loft three times, and then shot twice through the closet door behind you. One shot went wildly into the floor. I escaped from the rest room down there after jiggling the chair loose from under the knob, rushed up here to try to stop him, but I was too late. He had already shot each of you to death. But I caught him by surprise, wrestled the gun away from him, and then shot him in self-defense."

"Self-defense?" Andrea scoffed. "You shot him in the back. Forensics would prove that in an instant."

"No matter," Tim dismissed her contention. "I'll tell the police that as we fought and I wrestled the gun out of his grasp, he turned around to grab that broken broom handle on the floor to bludgeon me with and I shot him before he could turn back and hit me. So, you see, five shots through doors by him, one wild shot into the floor, that's six out of the nine. One shot at the end to stop your murderer and my attacker. That leaves just enough. One shot for each of you never to live to tell your tale."

Tim was about to squeeze the trigger when Danny stopped him abruptly.

"It won't work, Tim." He said calmly. "From way back when you were my associate, math was never your forte. Remember when you miscounted the number of kids going on the annual fall youth retreat? We were out there at the camp in Ligonier, and we had all the camp staff, our adult chaperones, you and me, searching the acres of woods for a kid who didn't exist? Eight shots were fired from that gun. You can shoot at one of us, assuming you can hit what you're trying to aim at. But even if you take me out, Andrea here is a former Michigan State Police Sergeant. And I wouldn't like your chances. Out of bullets, an enraged, out-of-control martial arts expert taking revenge for the shooting of her husband. You'd be better off using that last bullet on yourself. Put an end to your sorry life and misery."

"He's right," Andrea said just as confidently. "There were eight shots made. The initial assault by Frank wasted four rounds, not three. They were fired in rapid succession, so they blended together."

A definite seed of doubt was planted in Tim's moldy mind and took root. Mentally he tried to recount the shots he had heard. *I was sure that Frank fired three times at first. But I was just entering the sanctuary, the sound was somewhat muffled, and they did run together.* He kept swinging the gun from Danny to Andrea and back to Danny. *They have to be bluffing. They're desperately trying to confuse me.*

"You're both wrong. I have two bullets left, and each one has one of your names on it."

"You're the one who's wrong, Tim," Danny fired back with complete certitude in his voice and manner. "There's only one bullet. Face it, it's over. What's the sense of sacrificing your life at this point?"

Tim just had to know for certain. He kept the gun muzzle pointed at Danny but gripped the end of the clip with his left hand. He pulled it out of the handle of the Beretta to verify that there was in fact a bullet remaining in the clip, as well as the one in the chamber. He had just enough time to see that a round was still in the clip and shove the clip back in before Danny grabbed the broom handle off the floor and swung it like a baseball bat. It struck Tim's hand so that the pistol jerked upward, and his finger squeezed and fired the bullet in the chamber into the ceiling.

Danny had not succeeded in knocking the gun completely out of Tim's hand. So, he lunged forward and unleashed his best punch at Tim's face, striking him on his cheek.

"Run," Danny hollered at Andrea.

Since Tim still had the gun in his right hand, he would have been able to fire off the last bullet and kill at least one of them. Danny was right on Andrea's heels as she threw the door open and ran out among the choir pews.

Tim rolled over, scrambled to his feet unsteadily, a bit

stunned by Danny's blow. He was thrown off balance against a stack of boxes, regained his balance, and then dashed after them.

The two of them were scrambling down the choir loft steps as Tim ran out of the old study door. He refrained from firing off a wild shot at distance. *I'm younger than those two, and they still can't open the outer doors of the sanctuary without a key. I'll catch up to them and finish the job.* He ran as fast as he could through the choir pews and down the steps.

As he went, Tim mentally cursed himself for allowing doubt to be planted in his mind. Obviously, they had bluffed and there were, in fact, two bullets left when he felt forced to check the clip. Danny had taken advantage of the fact that it had always been in Tim's nature to question himself. His knowledge, his skill, his circumstances, and how he came across to others.

Damn them. But no matter. When I catch up to them out in the office area, I'll put this last shot into Danny's damn brain and use the empty gun to bludgeon his pretty wife to death. After you've killed two people, two more come easily.

Already he was gaining on them as he reached the bottom of the steps, and they were just making the turn at the door into the hall leading to the office area. He sprinted even harder and came to that door in time to see Andrea and Danny turn the next corner and head for the same outer door that Mildred had been going toward when she set her box of things down that last day.

Bad mistake, Henriks. Tim smiled grimly.

Tim Murphy literally never knew what hit him. As he turned the corner just behind Danny and Andrea racing toward the parking lot door, a massive arm clothes-lined him across his throat, lifting him off his feet, causing him to somersault backwards a full 360 degrees and land flat on his stomach, gasping and wheezing for air through his broken larynx. If it had been an action in a college or pro football game, it would have resulted in at least a fifteen-yard penalty against Will "Tiny" Jones. More likely an ejection from the game for such a dangerous tactic. But on this occasion the result was the complete incapacitation of a double murderer who had wanted to add two more to his score.

Danny had been right. It was over.

CHAPTER TWENTY-THREE

The force of the blow to Tim's Adam's apple was so strong that even Tiny had to rub his aching arm as he loomed over the fallen murderer. Behind him was Angela, alongside Andrea and Danny. Andrea had thought quickly and picked up the Beretta from where it had skidded against the hallway wall. She immediately ejected the last remaining cartridge from the chamber and pocketed the live round. Tim continued to gasp and reach for his damaged throat, twitching weakly on his stomach.

"Do you think we'll need to do an emergency airway puncture to keep him alive?" Angela asked.

"No, not as long as he's still taking in air," Andrea said. "Just let him gasp and choke for a while, until police and an ambulance get here." It seemed uncharacteristically harsh for Andrea, but she harbored deep resentment for anyone who tried to kill her husband.

Danny looked down the hall to the shattered glass door that exited to the parking lot.

"I see you had your own key," he said to Tiny, who was still rubbing his arm. A brick lay on the tile floor among what looked like thousands of shards of broken glass.

"Yah, fortunately it's a common habit of people to hide a key somewhere near an outside door. Although I think this one had actually been intended to prop the door open when people were carrying stuff in and out of the church." Tiny chuckled over his combination key and door stop.

Danny couldn't wait any longer for an explanation. "Okay, spill it, you two. How did you happen to come back here to rescue us yet again?"

"You know that's what I do," Tiny grinned and poked Danny in the arm. "I've been saving your sorry ass ever since that dark night in the parking lot at New Life Community Church, back up there on the Hill."

"Okay, I'll tell you what happened. Angela and I drove back over to Steel City Development and Design to try to make that play on Thomas Thornton as we had discussed. That young brother who's the security guard out at the entrance booth let us right in, although I think he was surprised to see us back after our getaway the last time."

"Anyway, we just marched right up to the reception counter and demanded to see the Chief Operating Officer, Thomas Thornton. I told the startled young receptionist that she had better interrupt Mr. Thornton at whatever he was doing, 'cause we wanted the fifty thousand dollars that was due us on the South Presbyterian Church deal. That we'd been kept waiting long enough. Well, she didn't know what to make of that demand, so she figures she better call Mr. Thornton and defer the matter to his judgment and authority."

Tiny paused for breath, and Angela joined in. "We knew that it was pretty gutsy of us, such a bold, frontal attack, but we figured that Thornton wouldn't want those under-the-table payoff bonuses broadcast among his lower-level employees there by the reception area. So, there was a reasonable chance that he would see us, if for no other reason than to find out just how much we knew. And to figure out how he could shut us up."

Tiny took back the narrative. "As it turned out, however, Thornton wasn't going to play our game. And he not only refused to meet with us, but he also told the Chief of Security to detain us while he called the police to report an extortion attempt. So soon two uniformed security guards rushed up to the reception area. But when they approached us, they looked at my svelte figure and radioed in for additional help on one of their little walkie-talkie units pinned to the shoulder." Tiny touched his own shoulder to demonstrate.

"We took advantage of their enhanced caution to exit quickly once again. The Town Car was still at the curb right outside the main entrance. Valets had been busy and hadn't yet moved it into a parking space. We jumped into our seats and took off. Once again when we reached the outer booth the arm was up, and the brother waved us through while he was speaking on the phone."

"Yah," Angela said, "probably reporting that he tried to stop us, but that he had to raise the gate arm to keep us from crashing through it. My honey knows how to make strategic allies." She smiled beautifully and rubbed Tiny's arm herself, tenderly and lovingly.

"And obviously you headed back here to the church," Danny said.

Tiny resumed his account. "Figured that was the best thing to do. As we were driving away from Steel City Development, I tried to call you two and got no response. And the first time that happened between us, Danny, I ended up having to make a long drive from Pittsburgh to Leelanau County, Michigan to find out why you weren't answering your cell phone."

"How well I remember, big guy. You really arrived in just the nick of time and saved my bacon that night."

"How many times do I have to tell you, slow learner?" Tiny grinned as broadly as he could. "That's what I do. I always have your back, and I always pull your ass out of danger. I provide full-service security."

"But really, Daniel," Angela spoke up again. "This being on the target end of a parade of would-be murderers and assassins has gotta stop. My sugar isn't getting any younger, and rescuing you is getting harder on him." Tiny had gone back to rubbing his aching arm now that Angela had released it.

"Listen to your best friends, Daniel," Andrea said. "I want this Murder Daniel Henriks Club to disband, cease and desist. Or I'm going to at least go back to packing my little ankle gun wherever we go in our old age. And I don't know that my arthritic right ankle is going to take that very well anymore." The other three laughed at her protest, but all appreciated the sentiment. It was high time that people stopped trying to murder Danny.

"I want to know at least one other thing," Danny said as he pulled the group back to the subject of how Tiny and Angela came to their rescue. "What motivated you to use your brick 'key' to bust into the church?"

"Well, we got to the church, pulled into the parking lot, walked up to the glass-paneled door, and it was locked. There were two older ladies hanging around, obviously wanting to get into the church, and they told us that they had a meeting in the church this afternoon but had arrived only to find the church locked up. They had gone around and tried all the doors they usually used. Same story."

"Now these nice ladies didn't turn around and leave because, they assured us solemnly, their Women's Mission Committee meeting was very important and this, after all, was their special meeting time. They assumed that any church staff here today had gone out for a late lunch or on an errand or something and should be back soon. And they would be sure to make a righteous complaint about having to wait outside to be let in. They further added that it had been, oh, fifteen-twenty minutes already."

"Well, I looked around the parking lot and of course noted your rental car parked right outside the door. Tim Murphy's Volvo was parked in the 'Reserved for Pastor' space. The ladies' car was parked next to yours, but there was also an old blue Ford in the back corner of the lot, and something clicked in the back of my mind. I just wondered if it was the same car I spotted outside the Starbucks yesterday near ours when we stopped by there. It had the same dent in the back fender, and it was too odd of a conjunction to be coincidental."

"And we all know that you don't believe in coincidences," the women said in unison.

"'Too odd of a conjunction?' Again, I'm impressed, brother," Danny said as he ribbed Tiny again about his growing vocabulary and terms of expression.

Tiny chose to ignore him and went on. "So, Angela and I assessed the situation. It just didn't feel right. You two were undoubtedly inside the church. Unless someone had driven off with you, probably not likely. And Pastor Tim was in there. But why would the church be locked up tighter than the proverbial drum and those poor mission ladies couldn't get in? Nobody answered a doorbell for either them or us. And whose old Ford was that, showing up again where you were?"

"Frankly, I had the same damn vibes going off in my head that I experienced when Slick and I were racing up the Leelanau Peninsula to find you, and that county sheriff's deputy pulled us over for speeding on Highway 22. I had this overwhelming feeling – call it a guardian angel's whisper if you want – that there was no time to waste, that we needed to get through that door, and NOW. So, I picked up the brick door stop and converted it into an impromptu key."

"I bet the ladies were aghast at that move," Andrea said, laughing at the mental image.

"They took it surprisingly well," Angela said. "Martha there turned to Agnes and said, 'Maybe we should have tried that. Our meeting is important, you know.'"

Tiny roared, remembering that scene of just moments ago. "Yah," he laughed, trying to keep talking, but having trouble. "And then Agnes there said, 'But what will we do now for a door stop?'"

All four of them just about lost it, almost forgetting the inert Tim Murphy lying feebly at their feet, still gasping for air.

"So, we entered through the new opening in the outer door," Tiny said, "although the two church ladies kinda hung back, wondering if they should follow us."

"But Agnes said to her buddy, Martha," Angela couldn't help but continue to laugh, "'Come on, Martha, this man obviously knows what he's doing. But he may need our help.'"

Tiny continued. "So, as the four of us pick our way over the shattered glass, Ang and I hear you two running like bats outta hell down the hallway from the sanctuary and headed in our direction. Now the only reason for the two of you to be motoring like that was if someone was chasing you. Like a madman with a gun, as it turned out. So's I got ready as you reached us, stepped forward, and lowered the boom just as Murphy here came around the same corner."

"At the time I had no idea it was him and was frankly damned surprised when I saw it *was* him flipped over here on the floor. But I must tell you, I never clothes-lined somebody that hard in all my football games over the years. Timed it just right. And it felt like I broke my forearm like I must have his larynx. But it was worth it. Another successful rescue of murderer magnet, Danny Henriks."

"And me too," Andrea said. "And we're mighty damn grateful, Mr. Jones."

Martha and Agnes walked over to join the group.

"But what I especially got a kick out of," Danny said, "was when Martha here stepped forward and hit poor floundering Tim on his head with her tote bag."

Angela added, "Yah, you said, 'I don't know what you've been up to, Pastor Murphy, but I do know that you have no business chasing this couple in our church with a gun. Shame on you.'"

The Henriks and the Joneses laughed as the diminutive Martha drew herself up to the fullness of her four-foot, ten-inch height and huffed, "Well, he should have known better."

The called-for police cars and ambulance were arriving out in the parking lot, emergency lights flashing and uniformed Pittsburgh Police officers bustling in to take control of the scene. It didn't take long for the sergeant in charge to sort out what had happened. Andrea immediately turned over the empty gun and the one remaining bullet. There would be interviews and crime scene investigations to conduct virtually all over the church. And of course, it was necessary to retrieve the body of the repentant but fatally shot Frank Lewis up in the old pastor's study.

It took a while, but eventually the Henriks and the Joneses were able to return to their suite at the Omni William Penn hotel for a refreshing dinner and a quiet evening filled with thoughts and words of thanksgiving, relief, and love.

There would be no sightseeing the next day, Wednesday, because all four of them had seen quite enough of the Greater Pittsburgh area for one trip. More rest and recovery was interrupted only by follow-up conversations with the police and some other necessary phone calls. More pieces of the South Presbyterian Church conspiracy began to fall into place, and there would be more arrests made in the very near future.

Tiny, Angela, Danny, and Andrea were extremely glad to pack up and get ready to drive back to the Grand Traverse, Michigan area on Thursday morning. It would be good to get home.

* * *

After an early morning start, Tiny, Angela, Danny, and Andrea arrived back in the Grand Traverse area late afternoon on Thursday. Despite the physical, mental, and spiritual fatigue from their intense six days in Pittsburgh, they agreed to freshen up at their respective homes and then meet for a late supper at 7:30 at one of their favorite restaurants, the Mackinaw Brewing Company.

Once seated and served glasses of "Missing Spire" late-harvest Riesling, they put in their orders. Both Andrea and Angela were just a little weary of salads and decided together to order fat, juicy cheeseburgers.

"I feel like being a carnivore after being intended prey for both Frank Lewis and Tim Murphy," said Danny. "I'm ordering a king-size cut of prime rib, medium-rare."

Angela looked up at the server and reflexively ordered for Tiny. "A double order of whitefish filets for the big guy here."

"Nope," Tiny corrected her. "A Caesar's salad for me, light on the dressing and the croutons."

"You have to be kidding," Danny said with his jaw agape. "No big plate of fish filets?"

"Hey," Tiny said, "look at this waistline." He grabbed the waistband of his pants and wiggled it back and forth with unusual ease. "Ang has kept me on the culinary straight and narrow. While we were back at the apartment getting ready to meet you here, I stepped on the bathroom scale and discovered that I lost six pounds on that trip. I'm a born-again believer. Big Tiny is on his way to becoming Not-so-Big-as-before, Tinier-than-before."

"Well, don't let that disappearing waistline make you waste away entirely," Danny said. "The world still needs Big Tiny. I know we sure do." Andrea nodded vigorously.

"I wouldn't worry too much," Angela said. "He's got a long way to go to be able to disappear when he turns sideways."

"Speaking of disappearing," Andrea changed the subject. "I bet Tim Murphy is going to disappear for a long time. Pennsylvania is officially a death penalty state. With two under his belt, and one particularly heinous, do you think the district attorney for Allegheny County will seek the death penalty when he's up for sentencing? You two know the scene in Pennsylvania better than I," she said to Danny and Tiny.

"I dunno," Tiny replied. "There's been a raging controversy, of course, about it for years in the Keystone State."

"In fact," Danny added, "ever since he came into office, the current governor has used his reprieve power as governor to halt executions."

"Personally," Angela said, "despite my feelings that some people don't deserve to remain on the face of this earth after some of the violent, bloody murders they commit, I'm opposed to capital punishment. Lock 'em up. Throw away the key. Life imprisonment without chance of parole. But let their lifespan be set by the Divine Judge of all, not human ones."

"Will we hear what's happening with the other members of the unholy conspiracy?" Tiny asked. "I mean, all those creeps were in it up to their greedy eyeballs. Tim may have been the one to push Mildred to her most unholy death, but even cursory investigation should uncover that Thornton,

Alice, Todd, Bernie, Alan, everyone with their hands in the money pot, were accomplices in poor Mildred's demise."

"I think we'll be kept well informed as to how the investigation plays out," Danny answered. "We have two advantages. One, I used to be a volunteer chaplain for the Pittsburgh Police Department. And even though my good friend, Sergeant Jim Bradley is retired now, I still have people there that remember me and will be only too glad to share information."

"And second," Andrea said, "I have some good connections from my Michigan State Police days."

"I should say 'good connections,'" Danny said. "Despite her own retirement, it seems my wife is known all around the country in law enforcement circles. It's not just in the Traverse City and Northern Michigan area that she's been written up as a hero cop. The National Association of Police Organizations – NAPO for short – has decided to give Andrea one of their 'Top Cop Awards' for this year. She'll be honored at their Top Cops Award banquet next spring at the Marriott in Washington, D.C."

"Wow, congratulations, girl," Angela said. "When did you find out? You hadn't said anything."

"Actually, the letter was in the accumulated mail when you dropped us off at home to change clothes and freshen up. It was a complete surprise to me."

"NAPO is the largest police organization in the country," Danny added. "Almost a quarter of a million members strong. That's my honey." He beamed.

"Back to the unholy ones," Tiny said. "You said Wednesday afternoon that you had heard over the phone that the police were busy rounding up the conspirators."

"You're darn tooting," Andrea said. "Danny's detective sergeant contact confirmed that they had scooped up Alice Nelson in her real estate office, meeting with some important client couple. True to form, apparently Alice tried to make the police wait while her people signed their life away on an offer, but they hauled her away. One officer on each side, grabbing her under her arms, while she hollered over her shoulder, "Keep signing. I'll be right back."

"The woman is relentless," Angela said. "She gives man-eating sharks a bad name."

"Man-eater is about right." Danny laughed. "Nate Nelson knew what he was doing when he got out of that marriage."

"And we found out that when Bernie was brought in for questioning, he protested that the scheme was all Tim and Todd. That he was merely an unwitting investor who was victimized for his money." Andrea went on, "But the funniest one was Alan Alderman of Steel City Development. They tracked him down in a Pittsburgh International Airport waiting area, trying to board a plane to Samoa. Imagine that. Samoa..."

"No extradition treaty with the USA," Danny and Tiny chorused in unison.

"Well, neither Sarah Brand nor Frank Lewis ever made it to Samoa," Danny said. "And now Alan Alderman has failed. It's just not a very good escape plan, I guess."

"That's a great idea," Tiny said with a raised voice. "The four of us should plan a tour of South Sea Islands in the Pacific and include a nice, long stop in Samoa. We could sit at a beachside cabana with big Mai-Tai's..."

"And the cute little umbrellas...." Angela specified.

"Have it your way," Tiny went on. "And we should lift our glasses and make a toast of remembrance to all the poor souls that have passed on due to the unholy villains in our lives."

"Including, and especially, Mildred," Danny said solemnly.

"Well, God and the angels forgive me for saying it,"

Andrea said, "but I would lift my glass and stick out my tongue at Sarah, Frank, Ken, Wes and Junior Smith, the Marichettis – father, son and nephew, that despicable bear poaching ring, Susan Sutherland and her unholy gang, Tim Murphy and his co-conspirators...and all their demonic ilk...and say, we made it here. Too bad you didn't...so sad...NOT."

In his traditional style of pastoral benedictions, Danny said, "And let all the people say..."

"Amen!"

* * *

God's Angel of Providence and Protection had been forced to employ extraordinary angelic power and resources to keep Danny, Andrea, Tiny, and Angela safe during their almost week-long stay in Pittsburgh. High-powered bullets had been deflected as they passed through wooden doors, narrowly missing Danny and, especially, Andrea. A determined murderer had been brushed off-balance and impeded as he furiously tried to chase down the Henriks and put an end to their lives. The conjunction of Tim Murphy and Tiny Jones at the corner of the church hallway had been a perfectly-coordinated example of God's *kerygma* – the divinely right thing happening at just the divinely right time.

The Archangel Gabriel had, in fact, been enlisted to project a powerful, revelatory message into Frank Lewis's sick mind, resulting in the epiphany that the Angel of Providence and Protection used to save Danny's life by bringing to a halt Frank's attempt to choke Danny to death.

The Angel of Divine Retribution had likewise been enlisted to direct and empower authorities in their amazingly efficient and relentless rounding-up of the Destroy South Presbyterian gang. As was almost always God's will, the angelic manifestations of divine will and power had acted through the created things and forces that God had in place on earth.

But Danny was especially right about one thing. There were no coincidences, no "accidents," no "lucky breaks" or fluke happenings. Everything that had happened was a matter of Divine Design and will, of divine cause and necessary effect. Human beings were bestowed with the fantastic power of free will to make choices and decisions for themselves. Whether they had any inkling whatsoever of the inevitable consequences that would be put into effect by those choices.

The dilemma of poor, even fatal, choices and decisions that resulted in self-destructive consequences had been a curse upon humanity ever since the original Adam and Eve story. But still the loving Creator worked patiently with the human creatures, so often rescuing them from the consequences of their terribly bad decisions and actions.

The Angel of Providence and Protection was kept so engaged on Earth – and in this case, with Danny and his loved ones – that it was a miraculously good thing that angels know no fatigue, frustration, or failure.

The years passed by, as they inevitably do for human life spans. As people so often do, Danny, Andrea, Tiny, and Angela would joke from time to time about "we're not getting any younger." And according to divine design and will, each of their times on planet Earth were growing shorter as they aged. But those days in Pittsburgh, and then back in their scenic home in Northern Michigan, they continued to be blessed by the providing and protective angel. Whether they paused to think about it as often as perhaps they should, it was God's will.

The End

EPILOGUE

When the author wrote the first novel in this murder mystery series, the Rev. Dr. Hall had only published articles in magazines. But he had an idea creeping around in what he likes to call "the jumbled stacks of shelves, where dust bunnies and the hunched over elves of inspiration shuffle in the back of his mind," for a possible murder mystery. At that point some years ago, he did not envision beyond trying that first book, *Death Comes to the Rector*. But after "Rector" made a bestseller list in Northern Michigan, he hesitantly decided to try another one, *Death Crashes the Wedding*. When "Crashes" surprised him by winning a Finalist in fiction in the annual The Author's Zone book competition, *Death Stalks the Forest* became the third in the Death Most Unholy series, also known as the "Danny and Tiny" series. Then a fourth, *Death Not Investigated*, was also a Finalist in the TAZ annual contest.

Death Not Investigated had been intended to be the final book of the series, but literally by "popular demand," a fifth, capstone, namesake novel was written and now published.

The author intended the five novels to be mysteries with twists and turns of "I didn't see that coming," and as fun to read, he hoped, as it was for him to write them. But more than that, they carried messages of love, lifelong friendship, loyalty, perseverance, struggle, and triumph. And all in diverse settings and challenges to meet.

For the author, and perhaps other authors as well, there

can be little so rewarding as having both entertained and, hopefully, enhanced the minds and lives of the people so kind as to read his books. Thank you for your support and connection through these pages.

ABOUT THE AUTHOR

The Rev. Dr. David Q. Hall and his wife, the Rev. Maxine, both retired Presbyterian pastors, live with their daughters, son-in-law, grandson, and two dogs, in Oceanside, California, after moving there from the Upper Midwest forest and lake country.

His parish ministry was with congregations across the country in Pennsylvania, Michigan, Iowa, Wisconsin, and California. He served in diverse settings, including metropolitan, inner city, suburban, medium-sized and small cities, small town, rural, and the North Woods.

In addition to the several books in different genres listed in this book, he pursues his love of writing by producing monthly newsletter columns, an occasional guest story in regional periodicals/anthologies, and every once in a while, a sermon as a guest preacher for a church. In addition to his books sold across the USA, he is humbled by having readers in Canada, the UK, Italy, Australia, and other countries.

He has been selected to be featured in annual literary festivals, especially the annual one in Oceanside, California, whose motto is Write On!